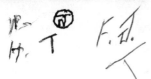

West of the Pecos

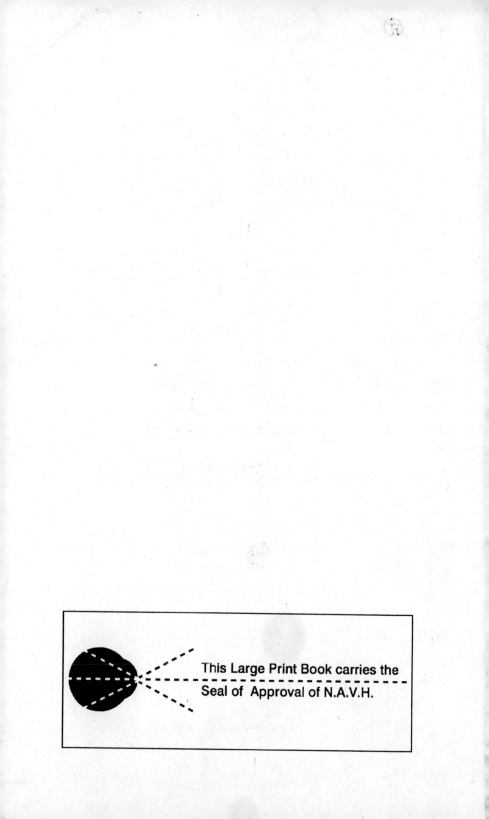

This Large Print Book carries the
Seal of Approval of N.A.V.H.

WEST OF THE PECOS

JACKSON COLE

WHEELER PUBLISHING

A part of Gale, Cengage Learning

GALE
CENGAGE Learning

Detroit • New York • San Francisco • New Haven, Conn • Waterville, Maine • London

GALE
CENGAGE Learning

Copyright © 1940 by Tom Curry.
Copyright © renewed 1968 by Tom Curry.
Wheeler Publishing, a part of Gale, Cengage Learning.

LIBRARY OF CONGRESS CATALOGING-IN-PUBLICATION DATA

Cole, Jackson.
    West of the Pecos / by Jackson Cole.
      p. cm.
    ISBN-13: 978-1-59722-807-7 (softcover : alk. paper)
    ISBN-10: 1-59722-807-9 (softcover : alk. paper)
    1. Large type books. I. Title.
    PS3505.O2685W47 2008
    813'.52—dc22   2008017937

Published in 2008 by arrangement with Golden West Literary Agency.

Printed in the United States of America
1 2 3 4 5 6 7 12 11 10 09 08

WEST OF THE PECOS

Chapter I
Pecos Death

The morning sun was turning from blood-red to golden as a gang of heavily armed men in leather, and wide, black-furred Stetsons, marked in front by a white circle enclosing an A, rode the chaparral trail west of the deep canyon of the Pecos River.

Their leader was huge of body. He had a bluff, tawny look to him. Under his dark hat was thick, sun-bleached hair, and there was a bulldog set to his heavy jaw. He was around thirty, and power showed in his proud, reckless carriage. He wore fine chaps over whipcord pants tucked into expensive boots, with long, cruelly-rowled Spanish spurs, a jacket of bull's hide, a fresh bandanna at his massive, pulsing throat. His thick nose and fishy, cold-blue eyes gave him a deadly air. The whole impression given was that of a man who will go to any lengths to gain his end.

"Hey, Aiken," one of his men sang out.

"Here comes Hawk! Hell-for-leather!"

Marshall Aiken, known as "Emperor of the Pecos," stared ahead as a rider came quirting full-tilt toward him.

The Emperor's bunched followers, with their mustangs' shoulders rubbing, chatted and smoked as they rode. They were hard devils, sloppy in dress, dirty and bearded, though their weapons were polished, gleaming, and ready for quick action. Some cast sullen, hangdog glares at their huge chief.

The man who had been called Hawk slid his mustang to a halt, beckoning to Marshall Aiken, who spurred out to join his lieutenant.

"C'mon, Chief," snapped Hawk. "We'll powwow as we ride. This is important! Leave the boys here."

Aiken gave the command, and the two trotted their horses through the narrow trail winding through the dense bush.

"Phil Gillette and Harry Purdue are over east, up on the valley rim, Aiken," growled Hawk. "We're goin' to drygulch 'em, here and now!"

John Hawk, Marshall Aiken's chief gunny and spy, was sinister rather than mighty. His body was lean and bony, and under the leather which acted as a shield from the tearing thorns of the Trans-Pecos growth, he wore a red flannel shirt and dark pants. His skin was several shades darker than Aiken's, and it was not from sunburn, for the high bones of his fierce face betrayed the Apache Indian blood in his veins. His hands were long-fingered, blue-knuckled, his lips sneering. Under his eagle beak bristled a crisp mustache, while his straight ebony hair reached his hunched shoulders. Sideburns swept down his hard-muscled jaws.

"What yuh found, Hawk?" demanded the Emperor.

"It's what *they've* found, and they've kept it secret, up to now! Lucky I been keepin' an eye on 'em. Phil Gillette's been against us, tried to stop his father from goin' along with us."

"That's true. But old Dave Gillette has agreed to market with us, buy supplies from us, from now on, ain't he? And he's got a lot of friends over this side the Pecos. We need Dave Gillette's backin'. Things've gone slower than the Guv'nor and me figgered. That old Hellcat, General Drew Simmons, has worked up Girvin town to fight us."

"Shore the townies are agin us!" snapped Hawk. "We've took their business, supplyin' the ranches, and marketin' their beef in Mexico. And still it ain't brought in cash

9

enough. My men won't fight, if they don't get their wages, and pronto. And without 'em, we're licked."

Aiken flushed. "I've done paid out all I had. I figger on makin' a loan from Dave Gillette. He jest got in several thousand for his spring herd."

"S'pose he won't lend it to yuh?"

Aiken shrugged. "He's got to."

"Thing to do is cinch it," growled John Hawk. "And what I've run on'll set us up for good. Only we got to keep it quiet, else there'll be such a rush over here we'll be swamped."

John Hawk quickly told Marshall Aiken what he had spied out. Dismounting at the top of a long tree-covered slope at the breed's signal, they unshipped their rifles and stole through the chaparral.

Hawk moved with Indian stealth, and Aiken stayed in his footsteps. They reached a low bluff, fringed with thorny bush, and peeked down at two young men who were squatted outside a black cavern mouth, hidden in the chaparral.

"Take Gillette," whispered Hawk. "I'll plug the other."

Steady, ruthless aim, and two rifles cracked. The victims keeled over without a sound.

A few minutes later, Hawk and Aiken, untroubled by murder, stole up and began to investigate.

They entered the cavern and were busy for over an hour. Emerging at last, they picked up the horses belonging to the dead men. Hoisting the corpses over the saddles, and fastening them with ropes, they started away.

"We got to cover this careful, Hawk!" declared Aiken. "If Gillette ever savvies we shot his son —"

"Look!" broke in John Hawk. "Over there!"

Aiken cursed as he stared across the wild chaparral. Only a mile off a group of cowboys were at work among a herd of cows. Some were looking up toward the height.

"Gillette's main crew!" growled Aiken. "Now we got to gun *them* out!"

"Yeah, they see us! Ain't no time to lose, Aiken! Hustle back and fetch the men. The Square G'll shore connect us with these shootin's. Lucky we got a couple spies in Gillette's bunch!"

Aiken spurred back to the fifty armed devils, part of his big army of hired killers. He snapped his orders to them.

"There's eight Square G men beyond," the Emperor told his gunnies. "Two of 'em

11

yuh savvy, Smith and Breen, was planted at Gillette's by Hawk. Be mighty careful not to plug them. The others get it."

With fighting to be done, the gunnies perked up. Eight to one. Such odds appealed to them.

The murderous gang galloped in Aiken's wake, and shortly came up on the little group of Square G waddies.

"Howdy, Aiken," sang out the foreman. "Seen Hawk and you up there on the hill. Who was that with yuh — seemed to be lyin' across their hosses —"

The gunnies crowded in silently. Marshall Aiken, eyes cold as ice, whipped out his six-gun and fired pointblank into the foreman's face. He was dead before he fell. Surrounded, the Square G waddies tried to get at their weapons, but it was too late. The gunnies massed upon them, pistols blasting at pointblank range.

Two were spared, for they were agents of Aiken and the Hawk, sent to Gillette's Square G ranch as spies.

Steers stampeded, mustangs snorted and reared at the clash of guns. But it was a massacre, over inside of a couple of minutes.

Overhead the sky was intense blue, the sun hot. Cholla cactus, with needle-sharp spines on deformed arms, green-and-yellow mescal, stalks thirty feet high, blazed with star-white flowers. The shadowy canyons of the Pecos region were purple in their depths, and the prickly pear, ocotillo, catclaw and bayonet found footing in the loose soil.

Here and there in this vast expanse showed the deep hue of pine forests, and bare red rock outcroppings. Through this great wilderness ranged wild horses and cattle, along with domesticated stock. Part of giant Texas, yet it was a world apart, an empire worth incalculable wealth.

And this land the Emperor of the Pecos and his killer band stained with the blood of his victims, victims of his insatiable ambition and greed. . . .

Up the west side of the steep Pecos canyon wall from the ford, Young Len Purdue urged his black mare. Water dripped off the sleek hide of the mount as she dug her hoofs into the red clay on the trail.

Twenty-five the month before, Purdue had long before reached man's estate, for he had taken care of himself for the past decade in a wild and rough frontier land.

He was lean of shank, though his shoulders were square and broad, with a good set to them. He wore leather chaps and a vest, and his blue shirt was clean save for drops of water which had splashed him as he had crossed the Pecos. He had let his mare swim the river, and a water mark now reached his hips, but he had held his guns high and kept them dry.

Crisp, curly dark hair, showed beneath his light-brown Stetson. His nose and mouth were good, and the jaw, pulled up by his tight chin strap, told of strength of character. As he turned in his saddle and looked back at the deep, dark Pecos canyon, his dark-blue eyes were sombre.

Purdue had received directions on directions as to how to reach the town of Girvin, on the east side of the Pecos, which divided this great part of still greater Texas from the other sections. So now, swinging south, he rode while the sun came up higher, and grew hot, yellow as gold. Now and then a long-horned steer would throw up its tail and rush, with a loud cracking "pop," from a draw into the dense thickets, or a jackrabbit would race the black mare, leaping back and forth across the trail for a hundred yards or so.

It was toward noon when he swung down into a deep but wide valley, and passed through a gate which had a square enclosing a "G" over it. Some low buildings were set along the creek bank — a house made of oak slabs, a barn and sheds, and horse corral.

As Purdue rode the black mare up to the front of the house, a girl came around from the other side and turned, looking up at him.

Purdue's heart leaped, for she was the prettiest girl he had ever seen. Her hair took the sun with a golden sheen, her eyes were brown, long-lashed and soft. She was small, with a little young figure, and wore a neat, freshly-washed blue dress. A ribbon of the same color bound her hair. Her lips were full as ripe cherries.

Purdue just gazed at her for a moment, because it was such a pleasure. Then he swung himself from his saddle, took off his Stetson.

"Howdy, ma'am. I reckon yuh're Miss Peggy Gillette. I'm Len Purdue, jest down from Kansas."

"Why you must be Harry's younger brother!" she cried, her voice soft and warm. "He has so often spoken of you!"

"Yes'm. I had a letter from him, tellin' me to join him." He stepped closer, looking into the brown eyes.

She held out her hand, and he took it, held it a moment, feeling the warmth of it. She dropped her long-lashed eyes, seemed a

15

little confused as she drew away her hand.

"Is Harry around?" Len inquired.

"No, my brother Phil and he have been out together the past week," she answered. "They're hunting."

Never had any girl stirred young Purdue so immensely. It was hard to take his eyes off her. He had been a little reluctant to join his brother since he'd have to leave a foreman's job in Kansas. Now he was glad he had.

"Come in and have a bite," Peggy invited. "We're just going to eat."

"Thanks."

The long-legged waddy trailed her up the steps, into the house.

CHAPTER II
"I'VE GOT TO PROVE IT!"

A stout, bulky man got up from a chair across the room, where he had been sitting by a window through which the sunlight streamed. He had to push himself with his hands, and leaned on a thick cane as he turned toward them. Purdue saw that he was lame, his right leg dragging stiff behind him. His bushy hair was graying, his shoulders bowed, and his beard was salted. But his brown eyes were an older, masculine replica of his daughter's.

"My dad, David Gillette," the girl told the visitor.

"Howdy, suh. I'm Len Purdue, Harry's brother."

"Glad to meet yuh, Purdue. Yeah, we're mighty fond of yore brother, my son Phil's pardner. Them two are up to somethin' — I dunno what. They keep mighty close-mouthed." He sang out, "Oh, Frank!"

From the rear of the house appeared a slim young chap of sixteen, light of hair, brown of eye, with the family look about him.

"My younger son, Frank," said Gillette. "Frank, this is Len Purdue. Show him where he can wash up, then we'll have dinner."

Frank was excited at meeting Purdue and having company. He talked all the time the cowboy spruced up at the basin on a bench outside the kitchen door.

"Do yuh know Marshall Aiken?" he asked, when he had run out of personal questions. "They call him Emperor of the Pecos around here. He's a friend of ours — comes here right often. He's goin' to lemme ride for him some day. He hires a lot of men, around two hunderd. He's shore boss in these parts."

"I heard somethin' of him in Girvin town," Purdue said absent-mindedly, for he was thinking of Peggy Gillette.

At dinner, Purdue's healthy appetite was doing justice to the hot corn pone and fried pork, when Frank cried:

"Hey, Dad! Here comes Aiken and a gang of his riders!"

Calls sang out, and there was alarm in them that sent dread sweeping through David Gillette and his pretty daughter.

"Boss! Boss!"

"That's Joe Smith callin'," muttered Gillette.

He got up, leaning on his cane, and limped out onto the veranda. Peggy quickly trailed him. Purdue and Frank left the table, too, and all stared at the procession that came down the valley toward the ranch-house.

Joe Smith, a Square G waddy, wild of eye, disheveled, rode up first, his crony Ed Breen at his mustang's heels. He flung himself from his horse.

"Boss!" he gasped. "A bunch of hombres from Girvin attacked us and shot down all but me'n Ed! They said you was in cahoots with Aiken and they're gunnin' for the Ring A! If it hadn't been for Aiken and his riders we'd've been massacreed along with the

rest, but Hawk and Aiken heard the shootin'
and come up on time to scare 'em off. They
run for the river and made the crossin'."

"Worse'n that," blubbered Breen, a
scrawny devil with reddish hair and deep-
sunk cheeks. "I hate to tell yuh, but — but
they got Phil, and Harry Purdue!"

David Gillette went white as a sheet. He
staggered, would have fallen had not Purdue and Peggy quickly supported him. Purdue, hearing the terrible news, was stricken
to the heart, hearing that his brother was
dead. But he sought to bear up, to help the
father and the girl crushed by this awful
tragedy.

Marshall Aiken pushed his horse up, swept
his black Stetson from his head. His face
was grave. In the background the Hawk
held the reins of the two horses on which
the bodies rested.

"I'm mighty sorry, Gillette," Aiken said,
as he dismounted. "We found yore son and
his pard not far from the Girvin ford. They
was drygulched, by Girvin men, I reckon."

Purdue stared at the big, light-haired
Emperor of the Pecos. Power exuded from
the great frame of the man. The stocks of
his Colts were smooth walnut, and he wore
them well in front.

"Who're you, mister?" asked Aiken, staring at Len Purdue.

"I'm Len Purdue, Harry's brother," the cowboy said soberly, and the pain in his eyes showed that the death of his brother had hit him hard.

Aiken and Peggy helped David Gillette inside to his chair. It was a terrible time for the Square G.

Purdue rolled a smoke, keeping a stiff hold on his emotions. His gaze ran over the crew in the black-furred hats, the Ring A men under the sinister Indian breed, Hawk.

"A tough bunch," he thought. "Look more like gunnies than decent waddies!"

Suddenly he found that the burning eyes of the bony Hawk were fixed upon him. He had a vague, inner warning that all this was not right.

"I'll shore check up on it," he thought.

John Hawk came sliding over toward him, a cigarette drooling bluish smoke from one corner of his lips.

"So yuh're Harry Purdue's brother," Hawk remarked. "What fetched yuh over this way?"

Purdue shrugged. "Figgered on joinin' my brother. Now he's dead."

"Reckon yuh had a letter from him huh? What'd he tell yuh?"

Len did not like this unpardonable curiosity. But he answered levelly.

"Said the range was big over here, and plenty of room, and for me to come."

"Well, if yuh want land, see us at the Ring A. My boss, Aiken, has all the say in these parts. You pay taxes to him, and we'll market yore beef for yuh and sell yuh all the supplies yuh need. West of the Pecos is run by the Ring A."

Purdue started to explode, but caution came to the fore. The Hawk had fifty men backing him, and Len was alone.

"Hell of a nerve!" he thought. But aloud he only said, "All right," and went inside the house.

Aiken was talking with David Gillette, speaking words of comfort to the bereaved father.

"Jest leave everything to me, Gillette," the Emperor announced kindly. "I'll send some men over to run the spread for yuh. I'll take charge of all yore business affairs and yuh needn't worry about nothin'."

Purdue watched the Emperor as he expansively played the big-hearted friend to David Gillette. He noted the glances Aiken cast at Peggy, whose eyes were wet with tears.

"Aiken's sweet on her," thought Purdue, and a pang of jealousy pierced him.

He didn't like Aiken and he didn't like

the Hawk. Both were hard customers, he decided. Gillette, broken by the death of his son, would be putty in the Emperor's hands. Len Purdue stepped over, held out his hand.

"I'm might sorry, Mr. Gillette. It's a hard thing to have to take. I'll be ridin' now, but I'll be back soon agin."

David Gillette took the waddy's hand.

"Yes, come back, Purdue. Too bad, too bad this had to happen."

"*Adios*, Miss Peggy," Purdue said to the girl.

She turned her unhappy eyes upon him, tried to smile. It was a pitiful effort. He shook her hand, and with a curt nod to Aiken, strode out.

The dead men were laid out on the porch, blanket-covered, and Purdue took a last look at the face of his brother. Then, steeling his nerves, he swung and went to his black, waiting in the shade.

As he was about to mount he found John Hawk, the breed, at his side.

"Leavin'?" Hawk asked softly.

"Yeah, I'm ridin'," drawled Purdue, "but I'll be back some time."

Men in black Stetsons lounged about, heavily armed followers of Marshall Aiken. Purdue swung into saddle and trotted his black mare out of the valley.

He knew how to read sign, and trailed back on the tracks left by the Ring A bunch as they had come in with their tragic news.

Several miles to the north of Gillette's place, he reached the spot where the battle had occurred, began casting about for signs. Dismounting he squatted down, peering at boot and hoof marks, at splotches of dried blood.

"There oughta be a trail of the Girvin men that come up on 'em," he growled aloud. "If what they say's true!"

Suddenly as he straightened up to seek that trail, a stinging bullet ripped the skin over his ribs.

He whipped out his Colt, whirling to face the threat from the rear. A second slug whizzed only an inch from his ear. He dropped behind a rock, and began shooting into the bush from which the fire came.

Blood flowed fast from his injured side.

"Can't stick here," he muttered, and at that instant he glimpsed, behind the sheen of a rifle barrel, a dark-skinned, fierce face. "The Hawk!" he muttered tightly.

Keeping his .45 spouting, Purdue jumped up and ran for the trees where his black mare was ground-hitched in a grove of live-oaks.

The Hawk's bullets came perilously close

as he raced full-speed. Then he was in the trees and, leaping on his mare, spurred off, protected by the thick trunks.

"That cinches it," he growled, looking back for pursuit as he sped toward the Pecos ford. "A hundred to one Hawk and Aiken done them killin's! But I got to prove it!"

CHAPTER III
OPPOSITION

It was dark when Len Purdue reached Girvin town, east of the Pecos, the jumping-off place for the vast lands claimed by Marshall Aiken.

The town was a typical Southwest settlement, with a square plaza in which cacti and bushes found footing in sandy soil. This was surrounded by frame and adobe structures — stores, saloons, a jail.

Purdue had only paused here before, to ask how to reach the Square G. Now he stabled his black and, after roughly binding his flesh wound, wandered over to a group of men in the plaza who were listening to a speaker on a flat wagon in the center of the open space.

It was an elderly man who was speaking, a man who, though along in years, evidently still had great fighting spirit. He was straight as a ramrod, and his eyes flashed blue sparks. His fine head was crowned by thick white hair, and a bulbous nose emerged from bushy white mustache, bearded cheeks and goatee.

Torches gave a yellow-red light, and there were some lanterns on the wagon platform. Three or four men sat on boxes behind the speaker who wore a ruffled white shirt, blue coat with a long double-tail, high black boots, and spectacles with gold rims.

"And I tell you, my friends," he roared, emphasizing his points by rapping his cane on the board floor, "we must crush this monster, the Emperor of the Pecos! I call on every man who can lift a gun to follow me when the time comes! Marshall Aiken illegally claims lordship over the vast Trans-Pecos. No man's rights are respected there. He collects taxes as though he held sovereign power, and his minions menace free citizens who seek to carry on their lawful affairs! He's a danger to Texas, and he's ruined this town!

"We got no more trade now, for Aiken forces folks over there to buy from him alone. No more cattle clear through Girvin, for Aiken markets 'em in Mexico. Some of you listenin' to me have fled from the

Emperor of the Pecos, as he's called. You can testify to his ruthlessness!"

"Say" — Purdue nudged a neighbor — "that feller's talkin' good sense. Who is he?"

"That's General Drew Simmons — fit under Stonewall Jackson," whispered the citizen. "He's workin' up oppersition to Marshall Aiken. Our town's dead as a doornail since Aiken grabbed everything across the Pecos."

Plainly Drew Simmons was a gentleman of the old school, a fiery Southerner who would fight and die for his rights. Girvin, once the main source of supplies for the great region over the river, had lost its trade, its wealth, thanks to Marshall Aiken's overweening ambition.

A stocky man got up from his box and stepped beside General Simmons. He raised a hand for silence.

"Who's he?" asked Len.

"Colonel Val Tydings, one of the General's chief helpers," answered his informant.

"Folks," began Tydings, "I want all of you who're willing to enlist against the Emperor, to give me your names. You know that with conditions the way they now are, the State of Texas can't send us much help. We've got to save ourselves, before it's too late. Girvin is shriveling up and dying, with all its trade

26

gone to Aiken."

Colonel Val Tydings, in his forties, had a stocky body and long arms. With his head bared, his carrot-hued hair glistened in the light. His eyes were keen, and his powerful voice easily reached Purdue at the back of the crowd. The colonel wore a brown suit, white shirt with dark tie beneath his strong chin, and he held a wide Stetson in a large hand.

A tall, cadaverous-looking fellow in a black suit that clung loosely to his skeleton frame, with sparse black hair and a bald spot, a sharp face, and deep-set black eyes jumped up and began to speak.

"Jest a minute, folks!" he shouted. "This here war talk's all mighty fine, but if yuh stop and think yuh'll remember Aiken's got over two hundred trained gunnies, besides Mex cowhands who run his spread. Attackin' such a gang'll take a real army."

This cold water was received by the crowd in silence.

"That's our mayor, 'Skinny Abe' Werner," Purdue's acquaintance told him. "He's a right smart thinker, too. Somethin' in what he says."

"Can yuh tell me if any of these fellers been across the Pecos today?" asked Purdue.

"Why, not that I've heard tell. Bad blood between us and Aiken's hombres, and it ain't healthy to ride over there."

Len Purdue had expected that answer. For him the story that had been told by the high-handed Ring A of the killings didn't hold water. And though he had only suspicions about who had killed his brother and Peggy Gillette's brother, he was ready to fight against Aiken and Hawk. He shouldered up to the wagon platform.

"My handle's Len Purdue," he told Colonel Tydings. "I can shoot and tote any sorta gun. Could I speak to yuh private a minute?"

Tydings studied him with his keen blue eyes. He leaned over, and Purdue informed him in a low voice of what had occurred across the Pecos that day, and of his suspicions.

"You may be right, Purdue," Tydings muttered. "We'll check up on it as soon as possible."

The tall, sunken-eyed Mayor Werner looked at them curiously.

"What's all this, Colonel?" he growled, but neither man answered him.

War clouds were gathering thick over the Pecos. Death was stalking the wilds of the Texas frontier. . . .

■ ■ ■ ■

Though Colonel Val Tydings had spoken truth when he said that Texas was too politically preoccupied to send effective opposition against Marshall Aiken, Emperor of the Pecos, there was some strength left in Austin.

A peg that held the tremendous state together, and not the least important, was Captain Bill McDowell of the Texas Rangers.

McDowell, a rugged old frontiersman, knew the ways of evil-doers. He had fought them tooth and nail, in his riding days, which now were over.

Pacing the mat, Cap'n Bill swore under his breath, biting at his ragged white mustache. Then as he heard a soft step he turned as the door slowly opened. A tall young man entered the office.

"Hatfield!" boomed McDowell. "Sit down! I want yuh to listen to this! Seems the worst yet! For it threatens Texas."

Though he was six feet tall, Captain Bill had to look up to meet the long-lashed eyes of Jim Hatfield, greatest of the Texas Rangers. Gray-green in hue, Hatfield's eyes would turn, when he was angry, to the coldness of an arctic sea. Splendid character was written in his pleasant face, too rugged to be called handsome. His skin, touched by the hot sun and winds, was a clear-toned bronze. A wide mouth broke the severity of his countenance.

His shoulders were tremendous, wide in proportion to his great height, and his torso tapered to the narrowing hips of the fighting man. The rippling muscles were like those of some great panther, waiting to spring.

Under his wide hat showed black hair. Long, slim hands hung easily at his sides, near the heavy six-shooters in their oiled, supple black holsters. Those guns could speak with the speed of a lightning flash, and many wrong-doers had learned that, to their permanent disadvantage.

But it was not only physical might and coordination of muscles that made Jim Hatfield great, the best officer Bill McDowell had ever known. He had a keen brain, and could use it. No better organizer existed, and he could size up a dangerous situation, decide on the right action to take in a jiffy. And he would take that action, come hell or high water.

More and more McDowell had come to depend upon him, and when he had a

particularly ticklish job that was too dangerous for most officers, he would send Jim
Hatfield.

Now Cap'n Bill was snapping the leash
off, turning this power of Texas loose against
the tremendous forces threatening the state
and its good inhabitants.

Hatfield listened as McDowell cursed sul-
phurously against the disturbers of the
peace.

"It's across the Pecos, Jim!" he rumbled.
"An old friend of mine, General Drew Simmons — we rode in the same company
under Jackson — wired me. I got other
complaints as well, against a sidewinder
named Marshall Aiken, who's set hisself up
west of the Pecos, and claims all public
range and rights there.

"Seems he's plumb ruined Girvin town's
business, takin' it for hisself. And Aiken's
got a big bunch of gunnies, doin' as he
pleases and collectin' taxes like he was a
sovereign ruler! Number of shootin's and
beatin's-up reported. He's got to be
stopped, before he gets so powerful he can't
be, savvy? That's Texas, and she stays so.
Yuh can contact Simmons in Girvin. He'll
tell yuh the set-up there, and yuh can ride
the river with him."

"Yes, suh," Hatfield said, his voice surprisingly gentle for so large a man. It was a soft drawl, and more than once had fooled an enemy into thinking the nature behind it might be soft, too, instead of being hard as steel. "I'll be ridin', then, Cap'n."

"Watch yore hide, Hatfield. They claim this Emperor is one tough hombre!"

The Ranger's jaw tightened as he nodded, shook hands with his commander, then went out.

Awaiting him was his magnificent sorrel, Goldy, sleek hide sheening in the sun. The horse was a proper mount for the Ranger, faster than anything that ran the vast stretches of the plains or climbed the pine-clad hills of the southwest.

The great golden gelding whinnied and nuzzled Hatfield's slim brown hand. These two understood one another. They had ridden the Danger Trail together.

Hatfield swung into saddle. His poncho was rolled at the cantle, stuffed saddlebags were across the saddle, and under one long leg showed a Winchester carbine in its saddle sling. Ammunition belts hung from the saddle horn with his lariat. Other belts, with loads for the Colts, were about his waist.

Then he was off, with Cap'n McDowell watching from the office window, feeling a lump in the pit of his stomach as he always did when he saw the Ranger ride off. For McDowell had his own memories of days when he had sashayed off on his law missions.

"If any man kin bring it off and live to ride home," muttered McDowell, "then it's Jim Hatfield!"

Chapter IV
To the Rescue

Days later, having made an incredibly swift run from Austin to the Pecos region in a bee-line Jim Hatfield shoved the golden sorrel toward Girvin town. He rode down a long slope, with high mesquite forests and scrub pines making black splotches in the night.

Stars twinkled thick as dust in the heavens, and the glow ahead must be Girvin.

The wind blew against the Ranger's strong muscled cheek. It rustled the dry pods of the mesquite, spurting tiny tornadoes of dust under Goldy's stirring hoofs. Suddenly the sorrel sniffed, shook his handsome head so that the mane softly flipped.

"Thanks for the warnin', Goldy," murmured the Ranger.

He slowed, keen ears alert, for the sorrel

had told him as plainly as in words that men were near at hand. The horse had caught some scent or sound imperceptible to human senses.

Looking down the rough slope in the wind direction, past the limits of a mesquite jungle, Hatfield sighted a couple of red-flaming pitch torches. As he pulled Goldy up, he saw several dark figures against the light in a little chaparral clearing.

"Now what are they up to?" he mused.

He left his saddle, touched the sorrel silently, caressingly, so that Goldy would stand quiet. Then Hatfield stole, silent as a wraith, toward the gathering.

Coming in closer, he squatted in the blackness of a thicket, peering at the strange scene. Half a dozen men in black Stetsons, which had some white design attached to the front, were lynching a victim who, hands tied behind him, sat a black horse under a tall oak, a horizontal limb of which would make a handy gibbet.

The man about to be strung up was young; a lean fellow in leather and Stetson. Hatfield could make out the firm set of the young man's face, and how proudly he faced the terrible danger, with death but a minute away.

So near was the Ranger that he could hear

what was being said. A bony, dark-faced man whose high cheekbones and straight black hair proclaimed him an Indian breed, was standing by the stirrup of the victim.

"Anything to say, before yuh kick the air, Purdue?" he growled.

"Only that yuh can go to hell, Hawk," the man on the black mare coolly replied. "Yuh dirty killer!"

John Hawk shrugged, and Len Purdue braced himself, as one of Hawk's killers tossed one end of a lariat over the oak tree limb. A hangman's noose was rapidly tied in the other end.

"Here, write this," Hawk ordered another of his gunnies. " 'This is a warnin' to men who fight the Emperor of the Pecos!' Pin it on the skunk's shirt."

The Hawk lit a cigarette as he waited for the crude sign to be made. In the match glow his face shone a burnished copper, and his dark eyes were slitted.

"Huh!" muttered Hatfield. "Don't seem like no vigilante gang! Reckon the Emperor of the Pecos is punishin' some enemy."

He knew men, could say from the aspect of Hawk and the hard devils around Len Purdue that they were not just hotheaded citizens about to take the law into their own hands.

35

Rapidly he flitted back to Goldy, mounted, and, drawing his bandanna up to mask his features, started for the lynch party.

John Hawk, the sinister breed, was holding the noose now, making ready to place it over Purdue's head. In a jiffy Purdue would be a dead man.

Charging toward the little clearing, Jim Hatfield uttered a war-cry that rang through the night shrill as a Rebel yell.

Hawk and his men whirled, reaching for weapons. Hatfield's big Colt roared, and Hawk went down, a bloody streak appearing on his cheek where the Ranger lead had burned.

Both guns out, Hatfield fanned the mob with bullets, shooting to rattle them or to discourage fight. They could not see him save as a dark wraith in the night, but they were silhouetted by their torches. Bullets ripped the air, hunting him, but he was moving at the full speed of the fast sorrel and though he heard the whistle of lead, and one bullet nipped at his sleeve, none hit the Ranger.

"Knock out them lights!" bellowed one of Hawk's aides.

Hatfield fired at a man who sought to douse the torches. The gunfire was deafening, and the lynch mob's horses, over to one side were dancing around, starting to stampede.

John Hawk came up on his knees, rubbing his face as though dazed. A slug from a Ranger gun burned his ribs as he sought to get out his pistols. The lean breed rolled over and over for the safety of the bush.

"Get goin', Purdue!" shouted Hatfield as he came abreast of the young fellow under the oak.

Though Purdue's hands were tied behind him, his black mare was free, and he touched her sides with his spurred heels. Ducking low, Purdue put the black at the dense mesquite thicket to the west.

"Stop him — shoot!" shrieked John Hawk.

A couple of the gunnies turned their weapons after the fleeing Purdue, but Hatfield slugs spurted up dust or tore the air so close to them they could not get fair aim. In seconds Len Purdue had hit the wall of bush with a loud *pop,* and was out of sight.

John Hawk's half dozen men scattered like chickens when a rock is thrown amongst them, diving for shelter. Bullets from Hatfield's smashing Colts cracked their nerve, and they could not see him, save for brief glimpses as the golden sorrel's hoofs pounded the earth, flashing past a narrow vista as he rode a circle of confusion around the lynch gang.

One torch had been knocked down and gone out, the other still flamed. All of Hawk's men, however, had made cover, several with bleeding creases from Hatfield's pistols.

"Get to them hosses! After him, yuh fools!"

That was Hawk's fierce voice urging them to catch the fleeing Purdue.

Hatfield pivoted Goldy and rode back, guns flaming. The killers were shooting at him, and the bullets zipped in the mesquite leaves or threatened him as they flew past in the night.

"Reckon that Purdue galoot's got a fair start," he muttered, low over Goldy as he rode hell-for-leather on the trail of the man he had rescued from a terrible death.

Spurring down hill, the Ranger left the scene. He had accomplished his purpose, which had been to snatch Purdue from the hands of the lynch party. Not yet aware of who his enemies were, Jim Hatfield had purposely refrained from shooting to kill. He had burned the would-be lynchers with lead, and got Purdue away. That was enough. It was not the Ranger's way to strike without full possession of facts.

He did not know anything about Purdue,

but the fellow he had saved was heading straight for Girvin town, a couple of miles westward. John Hawk and a pair of his men had caught horses and were coming in pursuit. The Ranger, still masked with his bandanna zigzagged as he rode, holding them back with his Colts.

For minutes the swift chase proceeded, Hatfield staying between Purdue and Hawk. Again he was hearing the shriek of lead that sought his vitals.

Across a cleared stretch he glimpsed Purdue, on the black mare, a shadow in the night as he rode full-tilt for the safety of the town. The young fellow looked around, and the Ranger bawled:

"Keep goin', Purdue! I'm all right!"

This seemed to relieve the fleeing young man's mind, for he spurred on, and Hatfield prevented Hawk and his gunmen from overtaking him.

Close to the outskirts of Girvin, Hawk called a halt, and after a last ineffective burst of pistol fire, the gunnies turned and rode back the way they had come.

Ahead lay Girvin town, and Jim Hatfield slowed, pulled down his bandanna mask, and replaced empty shells in his pistol with cartridges from his belt. Sliding the big revolvers into their oiled holsters, he swung around to the south, seeing that Purdue had gone straight into town and headed for the plaza where a group of citizens was gathered. They had been listening to speakers, but the gunfire had distracted their attention. They eyed Len Purdue keenly as he came up, hands still tied with rawhide to the horn.

Jim Hatfield made a wide circle and turned into a dirt road that led him into Girvin.

It was his habit to look over things before striking, and he had no desire to act the hero and claim Purdue's gratitude for having saved his life.

As Purdue hastily finished telling his story, citizens leaped on horses and started back eastward, evidently to hunt the lynchers.

Jim Hatfield rode slowly along a back alley, then swung up between the shadows of two houses, reaching a corner of the plaza where there was a watering trough. He dismounted, letting Goldy draw in a few mouthfuls. He spruced himself up, then looked over the town.

Len Purdue had been released, was being slapped on the back, congratulated on his narrow escape from death. Purdue kept staring eastward, expecting his rescuer to appear.

Leaving the sorrel under a tree, and rolling himself a quirly, Jim Hatfield sauntered toward the meeting.

"I tell yuh, he was alone!" he heard Purdue say. "One man pulled me outa that! Hawk and six more had me!"

"What'd he look like, this feller?" someone inquired.

"I dunno. Couldn't see him in the dark. Neither could Hawk. They grabbed me about an hour ago, behind the livery stable, when I rode in. Took me out there under the gun, questioned me some, then said I was goin' to die for buckin' the Emperor and opposin' him. They seem to know everything about us."

Shifting nearer, among the excited citizens, Hatfield regarded the men on the platform, evidently leaders in the community. One was an elderly man in a blue coat and ruffled shirt, back straight as a poker. His fine head was crowned by thick white hair, and his goatee twitched as he listened to Purdue's tale. Behind his spectacles his eyes burned with a fighting glow.

"You say Hawk did this?" he demanded in his deep voice.

"Yes, General Simmons. They figger I savvy too much about some things they've done."

41

So the old fellow was the man he was to contact, McDowell's friend! The fine-figured general swung and called:

"Colonel Tydings, suh!"

In response came a stocky man around forty-two, the Ranger guessed. He had long arms and carrot-colored hair. His deep-set eyes were keen.

"Yes, sir?" asked Tydings.

"Offer a reward of five hundred dollars for John Hawk's hide, dead or alive!" ordered General Simmons. "This kind of dirty business has to be stopped."

"All right, General. It'll be posted in the morning."

"Now looka here, General," protested a cadaverous man in a limp black suit, "we ain't got enough money to offer such rewards! As mayor of this town, I protest."

Simmons shrugged, impatiently.

"I'm in command here, Werner. The reward stands."

Hatfield hung around, listening. He learned much of the emotions of these people from their excited words. After a time General Drew Simmons left the gathering. It was time for bed, the general announced, and they had completed the evening's business.

Chapter V
Drygulching

Jim Hatfield trailed the straight military figure across the dusty road to a frame house, painted a dark red. Simmons went along the side alley and swung in through a door halfway to the rear.

"Who's that?" he demanded suddenly, as he quickly turned at a sound behind him.

Advanced in years as he was the general was not slow on the draw as he brushed aside his coat with his blue-veined hand. He brought out an old Frontier Model Colt, cocking it with his thumb as it rose.

"A friend," Jim Hatfield replied. "Bill McDowell sent me."

Drew Simmons had just entered his house and the door was still ajar as the Ranger slid up.

The general stood by the table, on which a lamp was burning low, facing the door. Jim Hatfield, hands in sight, entered and closed the portal behind him.

"Well?" Simmons demanded, deep wrinkles between his eyes as he regarded the mighty man who stood before him. He kept his gun ready.

"My name's Hatfield, Jim Hatfield," the Ranger told him softly. "Cap'n McDowell

43

says I can trust yuh. He sent me down on this Emperor of the Pecos business, Gen'ral."

Drew Simmons, an old warhorse of the Rebellion, studied the tall Ranger. No one could look at Hatfield and not be impressed by the power of the man, the tall strong body, the steady, cool eyes, the capable air of him.

General Simmons could judge a fighting man when he saw one and he knew he was looking at an ace now. Also, he caught the glint of the silver star set on a silver circle, emblem of the great organization known as the Texas Rangers. Jim Hatfield kept his star in a secret pocket until he was ready to announce himself. In that way he could learn more about the machinations of his foes than by riding around in the open, flaunting his badge.

"Set down, suh, and we'll have a mint julep together," General Simmons said. "I'd like right well to hear of Cap'n Bill. And I've heard tell of your exploits, Ranger Hatfield."

The general placed his pistol on the table, and Hatfield sat down. The room was a large square, with a thick carpet on the floor. There were chairs, a couch, and pictures, brought by Simmons from his

Virginia plantation which he had left at the close of the Civil War.

Simmons rang a bell, and after a minute a Negro man-servant answered.

"Fetch us two juleps, Sam," the general ordered.

He nodded politely to Hatfield, who went on to explain:

"I'm out here to put a rein on this Aiken hombre, Gen'ral. Cap'n Bill's in good health, and sends his regards to yuh. He said yuh'd give me a hand."

"Surely, Hatfield. Marshall Aiken must be checked. He's seized all legal power west of the Pecos, set up a state of his own there. He refuses to acknowledge allegiance to Texas. Mighty high-handed ways, too — shootin' and beatin', forcin' the people over there to pay him taxes! I, suh, owned minin' claims west of the Pecos, but Aiken's seized 'em. As for Girvin town, the merchants are done for, as Aiken has taken all our business."

"How many men can this Aiken muster?"

"Two hundred or more."

"Huh! Wonder where he gets the money to pay 'em reg'lar? And gunny wages come high."

General Simmons cast a sharp glance at his tall visitor.

"Most of the folks across the Pecos pay in beef and labor," he said, "but Aiken must need gold and silver to keep those gunmen satisfied."

Sam, the Negro servant, came in with a tray on which reposed two tall glasses garnished with green mint leaves. The general took one, raised it, and Hatfield followed suit.

"To the downfall of Marshall Aiken, Emperor of the Pecos," toasted Drew Simmons.

"I noticed tonight," said Hatfield, after drinking, "yuh ain't losin' time tryin' to bring that about, Gen'ral. Yuh're rousin' folks agin Aiken."

"Most certainly, Hatfield. . . . Er — suppose I call you Jim, my boy? I'm old enough to be your father. . . . Yes, Jim, Colonel Tydings and Mayor Abe Werner are helpin' me. We're enlistin' and armin' the best men we can dig up and when we're ready we'll cross the Pecos and crush Aiken. He's responsible for I don't know how many killings, and he's a traitor to the state, takin' advantage of the troublous times. He's even got a saloon and store at his Ring A, and the folks he controls are not allowed to cross the river. I'm planning the campaign and mean to have everything well fixed, not go

46

off half-cocked, though we must act soon as possible. Aiken grows more powerful every day that passes, and the time will come when it'll prove impossible to dislodge him —"

Jim Hatfield leaned forward, just at that instant alertly listening.

"Look out, Gen'ral!" he bawled. "Duck!"

He whirled in his seat, for his keen senses had caught the low click of a gun being cocked. It came from the side window opening on the alley. The draught was blowing the curtain there.

But it happened with stunning suddenness that sight, hearing and feeling were shattered at once.

General Drew Simmons threw back his fine white-haired head, his lips opening in a final futile gasp for air.

The julep glass fell from the relaxing hand of the old soldier, as his arms dropped. It shattered on the floor. Drew Simmons' head rolled over, and he fell forward on the table. On the ruffled white shirt front, a patch of crimson began spreading.

Swift as Hatfield was far ahead of ordinary men in the speed of his reactions, a bullet could not be driven back after it had started. Drew Simmons had been plugged through the heart by a skulking drygulcher who had crept to the side window and let go.

Whipping from his seat before the echoes of the first explosion had died, the Ranger plunged toward the table. That saved his own life, for a second bullet, designed for his vitals, tore across the small of his back, biting horribly, and the spasmodic nerve reaction sent him crashing heavily on his face.

He could feel blood spurting from the torn flesh, but his brain grew keener in danger. Despite his injury he thought clearly, and even as he rolled behind the thick-topped table, away from the death window, he knew he must get the light out at once.

In order to draw his Colts he would have to expose himself for a second, leaving him easy prey for the drygulcher at the window. Instead of attempting this, he tipped up the heavy mahogany table, knocking the lamp off it.

Bang! Rip!

The third explosion roared in the confines of Drew Simmons' living room. The bullet tore through the top of the table and plugged into the floor.

The light was out, now, and Hatfield heard a fourth bullet strike close to him as he rolled on.

He scrambled up on his knees and his

hand sought the feel of a walnut-stocked Colt. An instant-fraction later he was shooting at the window, his slugs tearing through curtain and glass, ripping chunks of pine from the frame.

The oil of the lamp had started to fire the rug, but Hatfield quickly stamped it out and ran toward the door, seeking the cowardly killer of General Simmons.

"Damn him!" he muttered, feeling the wetness of the blood that flowed from his torn muscles.

He was lamed by the wound, and some of his strength sapped, but he kept on going. He flung open the side door.

"Gin'ral, Gin'ral!" The inner door opened and the Negro servant, a lantern in hand, and a double-barreled shotgun under one arm, came in, eyes rolling in his head.

"He's dead, Sam," called Hatfield. "I'm in a hurry, but I'll be back." He started out, gun in hand.

Sam uttered a wail as he saw, by the faint yellow rays of his light, that the general was gone, slumped where he had fallen.

The shotgun roared, and the scattering lead pellets struck the wall and floor behind the Ranger, but Hatfield ducked outside.

Running toward Tin Can Alley, lamed by his wound, he gritted his teeth as he sought the man who had slaughtered General Simmons. Reaching the back of the house, he slowed, looking up and down. Then he heard hoofbeats, and glimpsed a dark figure, low over a horse, rounding a building at the end of the row.

"Halt!" he roared, and fired a quick one. But the moving horseman was racing out of his sight. The only reply was a lead pellet, that whistled over Hatfield's head.

"Hafta git Goldy!" he muttered. "Mebbe I kin rout him out."

He loped for the main street despite the jabs of pain from his hurt spine. But as he neared the side door of Simmons' home, a crowd of citizens came rushing toward him, blocking him. They saw the pistol in his hand, and a shout rose on the night air.

"Hey, there! Drop that gun!"

In the lead was a big man with a black beard and fierce eyes.

"Take it easy," called the Ranger, as they pounced toward him.

The old Negro, Sam, suddenly stuck his head out the door.

" 'At's him, Mistuh Chock!" he cried. " 'At's de man shot de Gin'ral!"

"What!" shouted Dan Chock, the black-bearded giant. "General Simmons is shot?"

"He's wuss, Mistuh Chock — he's dead,"

sobbed Sam. "He was sittin' in dere wid dat big debbil when suddenlike I hear guns!"

Cries of rage rose in the throats of Drew Simmons' friends. Back to the wall, Hatfield stood, falsely accused.

Several leaped inside, to stare at the body of their chief.

"Dead, all right," growled Chock, coming back outside. "Plumb through the heart, gents."

"Let's string this skunk up, here and now!" snapped a tall fellow with a bald head.

"Keep yore shirts on," ordered Hatfield. "While yuh're wastin' my time, the real killer is gettin' away. He shot through that side winder while I was talkin' with the general."

"Here come the mayor and Tydin's!" someone else sang out. "They'll savvy what to do."

Colonel Val Tydings and Abe Werner pushed to the fore.

"What's all this, boys?" demanded Werner.

"Sam says this big jigger killed the general," explained Dan Chock.

"The general?" shouted Tydings, stunned. He passed a hand dazedly across his eyes. "Our chief — dead?"

"As a doornail, Kunnel," whimpered Sam. "He was sittin' in de parlah wid dis big feller, drinkin' juleps, when guns popped."

Growls of rage arose, guns appeared in the hands of bunched citizens facing Hatfield. The tall Ranger could not shoot such folks, but he would not surrender, either, for they were working themselves up to lynch fury.

"Yuh'll pay for this!" screeched Mayor Abe Werner.

"Put up your guns," ordered Tydings, eyes on Hatfield.

"Yuh're all wrong, gents," insisted the Ranger coldly. "I didn't shoot the general. A drygulcher done it. He fired through the open winder, like I said. See for yoreselves. He wounded me across the back."

"Don't let him lie out of it," snarled Chock. "He must be a spy for Aiken. They sent him here to kill Simmons."

"String him up!"

"Take his guns!"

Hatfield stared at Val Tydings as the shouting rose higher. The level gray-green gaze met the firm eyes of Simmons' aide. The Ranger had a .45 Colt in one slim hand, and another in its holster at his hip.

Tydings swung, raising a large hand.

"Easy boys. We'll check up on what he claims. Fetch a torch. Let's look under the window."

Chapter VI
Attack in the Night

When a light was brought, Hatfield squatted, peering closely at the dirt under the opening.

"No heelmarks," he grunted.

But he knew, from the flat, pressed footprint he could barely make out, that the drygulcher had worn moccasins. This was not surprising, for the high-heeled, spurred riding boots of Westerners were no good for running or for moving quietly. Many men carried Indian moccasins to slip on in place of their boots when needed. Hatfield himself had a pair in his saddlebags.

He pointed with his gun barrel at holes in the window frame, at fresh gashes where the red-painted outer wall had been ripped to splinters. Glass, shattered from the pane, lay on sill and earth.

"Whoever shot Drew Simmons," he growled, "stood here, and fired between the curtain and frame. Then he run back, hopped on a hoss, and got away."

The wound in his back burned, the shock had been serious, but he had control over his keen faculties. He picked up a small object from the trodden dirt.

"What's that?" demanded Tydings.

Hatfield brushed the earth from it. It was a black cloth button.

Mayor Abe Werner uttered a curse. "Why, that's off my coat!"

Eyes swung toward the cadaverous mayor.

"Yuh can't blame it on me, gents!" he growled. "I was across the plaza!"

More men were coming up, and Tydings led the way into the room. A light had been brought that showed the dead Simmons as he had fallen. Hatfield let his Colt slide back into its holster. Finding of the black cloth button had turned attention from him for a moment.

The Ranger recognized Len Purdue, the young chap he had snatched from Hawk's lynch party. Purdue looked capable, like a good fighting man. His shoulders were square, his jaw strong. Hatfield took in the straight mouth, the sombre, dark-blue eyes, and ticketed Purdue as a future assistant in the battle against Marshall Aiken, Emperor of the Pecos.

The men of Girvin were checking the tall stranger's story.

"It does look as if there had been a duel," Tydings remarked. "Abe, how do you suppose your button happened to be there?"

Werner shrugged. "Simmons and me were friends," he said. "Mebbe I dropped it when

I was here after supper for a drink. I dunno."

Hatfield had a minute, while they were watching Werner. He touched Purdue's shoulder and the tall waddy swung, scowling at him, for he believed, as did so many, the big man must have shot Simmons.

" 'Anything to say, before yuh kick the air, Purdue?' " the Ranger said in a low voice. And added, quoting Hawk's words to Purdue when the cowboy was about to die; " 'This is a warnin' to men who fight the Emperor of the Pecos.' "

Purdue's dark-blue eyes suddenly glowed.

"By hell, 'twas you saved me!"

"I couldn't let 'em lynch yuh."

"What's all this about? You didn't kill Simmons?"

" 'Course not. I was sittin' here with him, and got wounded myself. The drygulcher got away and rode off north."

Tydings, frowning, turned back and stared at Hatfield. Hard glances came the stranger's way. Deep suspicion was still directed against Hatfield.

"I figger this gent's tellin' the truth, Colonel," Purdue spoke up. " 'Cause jest after I heard them shots, I seen a man ride like hell out of town, from Tin Can Alley. It must've been the killer."

Purdue's information cooled them off

some, and Hatfield's wound, as well as the bullet holes in the window and wall finally convinced them he was speaking truth. The black button, admittedly Abe Werner's, also shook their conviction.

"All right," grunted Val Tydings. "What's your name, hombre, and where you come from?"

"They call me Hastings," Hatfield answered glibly. "Jim's the first handle. I rode in from the Territory tonight and called on the General, who was a friend of my dad's. Reckoned he'd get me a ridin' job in these parts."

"Well, Hastings," ordered the colonel, "stick around town. Don't try to leave, understand? If you want a job, you can sign up with me, to fight the man who claims the Trans-Pecos."

"I'll do that, Colonel."

Hatfield left with Purdue, passing through the armed citizens. He limped beside the waddy, fighting off the pain of his wound.

"C'mon, and let's have a look at that wound of yours," said Purdue.

He took the Ranger to a shack across the plaza, where he cut away the ruined shirt and exposed the furrow the slug had made.

" 'Tain't so bad," Len Purdue said, "but it's messy and it shocked yuh. Wait'll I get some hot water and I'll ease it."

While waiting for water to boil, and having collected clean cloths, Purdue gave the tall man a cigarette and they smoked together.

"I'm right grateful to yuh for snatchin' me from Hawk and his gang," Len told him. "They grabbed me after dark and took me out there. Yuh was all alone when yuh saved me, wasn't yuh?"

"Yeah. They sorta got rattled, that was all."

"No, it was a mighty brave thing. Yuh got plenty nerve, Jim."

"Forget it. When you remembered seein' that hombre ride off, yuh returned the compliment, Purdue."

"Well, I had to back yuh up, Jim," Len said, grinning sheepishly. "And I don't believe yuh shot Simmons."

"What I told yuh is the truth."

Half an hour later, feeling better with his wound washed, and a clean bandage strapped across his back by the deft fingers of Len Purdue, Jim Hatfield limped up the main street of Girvin and went with his young friend into the Bull's Head Saloon, where they had a drink together.

Purdue told him more about the Emperor of the Pecos, of his suspicions against Aiken and the Hawk, and what had occurred at the Square G. He described the Gillette place, and Jim Hatfield did not miss the tightening of his face as he spoke about Peggy Gillette.

"Aiken's got the inside track, though, I reckon," declared Purdue. "She's mighty beautiful, Jim."

"Funny about that button off Werner's coat, near the winder," the Ranger said ruminatively.

Purdue shrugged. "Werner's a queer duck. He's always throwin' cold water on our plans. Jest the same, Simmons seemed to be a pard of his, and Tydin's trusts him. But Aiken's shore got spies in this town. Seems to savvy every move we make."

Hatfield had lost the aid of General Drew Simmons, but he had gained Leo Purdue. The anguish in his back was subsiding, and though he felt sore and stiff when he moved, he could stand it. He had the faculty of overcoming physical pain.

"Guess a trip over to this Ring A's in order," he mused, as he listened to Purdue.

Later he returned to the shack Purdue was using, near the town hotel, which was owned and run by Mayor Werner. He accepted Len's offer of the spare bunk.

They were quickly asleep, and the Ranger made up for lost time. He awoke, however, after several hours. Some innate warning brought him up alert, and his Colt was in hand as he raised on one elbow, listening.

The stealthy sound of footsteps was so faint that he thought for a time it was imagination. Then he heard someone at the door, seeking to raise the latch noiselessly.

Silently he slid from his bunk. Purdue was sound asleep, snoring. Jim Hatfield slipped across to the door as it was slowly pushed inward.

Against the faint light of the sky he saw the dark figure of a man, and the dull glint of metal on a revolver.

"Throw 'em up, hombre!" he snapped.

Convulsively the man jerked back. Hatfield's Colt roared, to beat the swinging pistol of the sneak, and the fellow folded up on the sill.

But there were more outside. Guns began to flash in the night, and bullets zipped around Hatfield as he crouched to one side.

He touched another enemy with his stinging lead, and the would-be killers in the night ran around the shack. They had horses waiting, and the beat of hoofs rang out as they sped away.

"What the hell's wrong!"

Len Purdue, leaping up, struck a match and touched it to the blackened wick of a candle. The little flame flickered, to show the dead man lying half in, half outside the cabin door. Hatfield leaped to the door, rolled the body over, staring at the hard face. A black-furred Stetson with the Ring A insignia, was strapped to the man's head.

"One of the Hawk's gunnies," growled Purdue. "After me again!"

Hatfield realized the futility of pursuit. The intruders were already gone.

"Reckon mebbe they counted on killin' two birds with one stone," he drawled. "Fetch that light outside here, Len."

It was pitch-dark, around three-thirty. With the candle, the tall Ranger hunted in the dirt near the shack. Some heel marks showed, but it was the track of a wide moccasin that held him.

"Shore looks like the one outside Simmons' winder," he mused.

His keen eye caught the glimmer of a tiny object, and he picked it up between thumb and forefinger.

"What's that?" asked Purdue.

It was a little white bead, of the sort used to trim an Indian moccasin. Hatfield carefully placed it in his pocket, and went back inside.

"What's up now?" asked Len, as he saw his friend pulling on his boots.

"I'm ridin', Len. And if yuh'll take my advice yuh'll sleep in the chaparral after this, and a different spot every night!"

"Yuh're right, Jim. I'll hafta be mighty wary."

"Yore idea that Hawk and Aiken killed yore brother and young Phil Gillette, and massacred them Square G waddies, is prob'ly right, but keep yore trap shut for the time bein' and we'll root it all out when the right moment shows. Watch yore hide. I'll need yuh."

All Girvin was excited. Hatfield was sure that he could accomplish little by hanging around the settlement, so figured on making his survey of the enemy first, and returning when he had all his facts.

"Yuh ain't leavin' town, are yuh?" asked Purdue, as the Ranger headed for the door.

"Pronto."

"But Colonel Tydin's asked yuh not to."

"Well, he'll jest have to stand it till I get back," Hatfield said dryly. "*Adios,* Len, and good luck."

CHAPTER VII
UP FROM THE BORDER

Hatfield hustled outside, in the cool of the night. Soon the dawn would be here, and he wanted to be on his way before the light of day. For what Purdue had said was true — spies were in this town, emissaries of Marshall Aiken, Emperor of the Pecos.

He saddled the golden sorrel and, throwing his long leg over leather, trotted Goldy out of the town.

The motion jolted his injured back, but after awhile it loosened up. Heading for the ford across the Pecos, he descended to the river by way of a steep dirt trail. The sorrel waded in and started swimming. The current pushed the powerful animal down, but Goldy got his footing on the other shore and, wading up the shallows, started the climb to the western heights.

Before the dawn lightened the wild lands, Jim Hatfield was well into the jungle of mesquite and cactus growth, pushing toward the Ring A, Aiken's stronghold. From Len Purdue he had learned that the Emperor was hiring more and more fighters, to balk the attempt of the Texans to crush him.

In his mind was a dangerous plan, but the sort he enjoyed putting into operation.

That afternoon, as he rode under a hot, brassy sun for the Ring A, his appearance had changed. His clothing was smeared with clay streaks, he had crunched in his Stetson, and he hadn't scraped the beard stubble from his face, also dirty with reddish specks of dirt. Sloppy in appearance now, as though careless and in from a long run, he rode loose in his saddle. His hat was cocked on one side, and all in all had the look of a tough gunny. Jim Hatfield knew how to act a part, and that was what he was doing as he headed for the stronghold of Marshall Aiken, Emperor of the Pecos.

"Reckon we can learn plenty over here. Goldy," he told the sorrel.

The rolling hills extended in a breathtaking sweep before him. From the high trail he was riding he could look down on the blue waters of a big lake, an artificial reservoir, with a dam at its southeast end in a narrow gap.

The keen, gray-green eyes took all this in. The deep-walled ravine that wound below the dam interested him.

"Why, yuh could shore wash an army outa there, if yuh let loose that dam," he thought. "Ketch 'em in there, mebbe lead 'em through —" He shrugged. "It'd take dynamite to blow the dam."

He rode on, observing the land, and near dark came to the gates of a great enclosure, the home ranch of Marshall Aiken, marked by a triangular white A in a ring. A gunny challenged him, rifle in his hands.

"Where yuh goin', hombre?"

Jim Hatfield acted the role he had undertaken, that of a gunman hunting a job. A piece of plug tobacco shoved in his dirtied cheek distorted his mouth. He was sloppy in the saddle, guns riding in front. He looked the part, all right.

"Is Hawk here?" he growled, scowling at the armed guard.

"Naw, he ain't. What yuh want of him?"

"Well, I heard tell he was hirin' fightin' men. That's me, shore enough."

"So yuh're huntin' a job?"

"Uh-huh — but seems to me yuh ask a hell of a lot of questions," snapped the tall stranger, imitating the ticklish temper of a desperado.

"No offense. Ride on up the lane and round the big house and ask for Shorty. Tell him what yuh want."

Hatfield shrugged, let Goldy trot toward the buildings.

The main house was immense, spreading out from a central section in half a dozen radiating wings like the spokes of a gigantic wheel. Chimneys stuck from the whitewashed roof, but the adobe brick from which the house was built was painted. Wide verandas ran around the place. It was the home of a frontier king.

"Shore spreads hisself," thought the tall Ranger.

There were other structures, barns and stables, a huge bunkhouse, windmills, corrals. Great bands of horses were in fenced pastures. Blooded stock was held in stables. Workers and fighters were about, and Mexican servants, who evidently did the cooking and cared for the place.

Off to one side was a building marked "Store and Saloon." Here, the feudal Emperor of the Pecos sold supplies and liquor to his subjects, making a tidy profit for himself, and at the same time cutting out Girvin.

Toward the back of the main home, Hatfield was again challenged. "I wanta see Shorty," he said.

He found "Shorty," a vicious looking, broad and bow-legged gunny, leaning back in a chair against the front of the bunkhouse.

"I'm up from the Border huntin' work," growled the Ranger.

"A ridin' job?" grunted Shorty, peering at him from beneath bushy brows.

Hatfield dismounted, stood holding his reins, the sorrel drooping his head.

"Yeah," drawled the Ranger. "And I don't

care for chasin' dogies, either."

"That ain't the reg'lar punchin' job here," Shorty told him laconically.

He licked his thick lips, frowning. His low forehead and sandy hair showed under his wide black-furred hat, shoved back on his bullet head. At some time he had had his nose broken, smashed in against his face, but whether this was a blemish or an improvement it would have been difficult to say, for Shorty was no beauty, and his yellowed buck teeth were no accident.

"Do yuh think I'd've rode all the way up from the Rio if I figgered yuh'd set me to nursin' cows?" Hatfield asked coldly.

"Can yuh shoot?" Shorty asked, winking at other gunnies who were lounging around, some in the long bunkhouse, others outside.

For reply, Hatfield drew a six-gun and fired from the hip without seeming to take aim. His slug drove a nail into the post of the corral fence.

"Yuh aim at that nail?" demanded Shorty, unbelievingly.

"See the one jest above where it was?"

"Yeah, I see it."

The Ranger let go again, easily, with no aim that Shorty could notice. The nail head disappeared and in its place was a bullet hole.

"Some shootin'," admitted Shorty, with new respect.

"Yuh're hired, gunny," a cold, deep voice said from behind them.

Jim Hatfield slowly swung, letting his six-shooter slide into its supple holster.

Big as Hatfield was, he looked on a level into the icy, pale-blue eyes of a giant who had come up quietly. The man was bare-headed, exposing coarse, thick, bleached hair. The heavy bulldog jaw stuck out. He wore fine clothing, and boots that would cost over a hundred dollars with their silver, hand-carved spurs. Hatfield took in the bear body, curving lips and thick nose, the cruelly cold fish eyes.

He knew he was looking at power, and that the slightest mistake would cost him his life.

"This is the boss, Mister Marshall Aiken," Shorty said.

Having ridden straight to the heart of the enemy's camp, posing as a gunman looking for strong-arm work, Jim Hatfield faced Marshall Aiken, the man known as Emperor of the Pecos.

Aiken's cold glance went up and down the great Ranger's figure, and he seemed approving. Hatfield, though he had made himself appear sloppy and tough, was a real fighting man, as this was Marshall Aiken's primary consideration in hiring quick-trigger artists. The new "gunny" passed inspection.

"Thanks, Chief," growled Hatfield.

"Stick around," ordered the Emperor. "Shorty'll tell yuh what to do. What yuh call yoreself, big feller?"

"Make it Sonora Jim, *this* time, Chief," mumbled Hatfield, because of the tobacco cud that bulged his cheek.

Aiken's lips smiled though his eyes did not warm. The Emperor was a dangerous customer, and a clever one, and Jim Hatfield decided that he would probably be watched, spied on, until he had proved himself.

"Ain't Hawk back yet?" Aiken asked Shorty.

"No, he ain't. Mebbe he had trouble catchin' Purdue."

Aiken scowled at Shorty, shrugged, and went back to the big house.

"C'mon, Sonora Jim," Shorty said, "and I'll interduce yuh around some."

With the bow-legged lieutenant, Hatfield strolled about meeting hard-eyed, wolfish men whose gun stocks were worn smooth from constant use. There were Mexicans in wide red sashes and bespangled velvet pants, with great sombreros of black felt on their dark heads. They favored the long knife, though they also carried pistols. There were Border ruffians, devils who would kill a man to see him kick.

The Ranger, slouching along, maintained his own hard pose, carelessly nodding to each one Shorty pointed out. But his keen eyes ticketed every face, to be able to identify a future antagonist.

"Let's have a drink," invited Shorty, and they sat at a table in the long bunkhouse, and poured out whisky.

Gambling went on, and boastful talk, although most of these men had a price on their heads somewhere and were purposely vague about their past. Hatfield's size, as well as the shooting bee he had put on, made them fairly respectful of him.

A meal was served, and the gunnies lounged around, smoking. After dark fell, there was a stir up front and several dust-covered, weary horsemen came along the lane.

CHAPTER VIII
PECOS EMPIRE

Shorty and several others went out, and Hatfield trailed them. In the light of big porch lamps he saw John Hawk, the lean, sinister breed, and his hombres. The bunch that had captured Len Purdue had returned from across the Pecos.

The breed looked worn to a frazzle. His cheek had been singed by a Ranger slug, and his ribs, too, had been injured by Hatfield's fire when he had rescued Purdue.

He dismounted stiffly, waved away his men, who also showed the effects of battle, and started up on the veranda. Aiken stalked out.

"It's about time yuh got back," he growled. "Did yuh take care of Purdue?"

Hawk spat venomous curses, his eagle beak twitching.

"We caught him," he snarled, "and jest as we were goin' to string the dog up, some pard of his gunned us in the dark and he got away."

"Yuh damn fool!" snapped Aiken. "You let him escape?"

"I couldn't help it," Hawk said sullenly. "I near got killed. Two wounds."

"Who done it?"

The Hawk shrugged. "It was night, I tell yuh, and we couldn't make out who it was. But he was one hellion of a scrapper."

"Huh! Yuh command two hundred fightin' men and yuh let one heller bust yuh! And

70

where yuh been all this time? Over at Gillette's, I s'pose, moonin' 'round my gal?"

Hawk swore again.

"We had to lie up for hours, before we were able to ride," he grumbled, "and then we couldn't cross the river till we saw a chance."

"Did yuh see the Guv'nor?"

"Naw, he was busy. Anyhow, everybody knows me. I couldn't get near town. Purdue got 'em all worked up against us."

"C'mon in, then. We'll have a drink."

Shorty sang out, as Hawk started after Aiken, "Hey, Hawk! Got a new man for yuh, and a good one."

The evil-faced breed swung, scowling. "Keep it till mornin', Shorty."

As Hatfield went back to the bunkhouse with the men, he was well aware he was being chaperoned. They were taking no chances.

He turned in early, for he needed rest. Before he fell asleep, however, he caught a snatch of talk between Shorty and another hombre.

"That there General Simmons," remarked Shorty's crony, "is gettin' together a right big force agin us, Shorty."

Shorty laughed. "If yuh knowed what I do, Vern, yuh wouldn't worry. It's all

71

planned to wipe them fellers out complete."

"Yeah? How so?"

"I ain't allowed to say. But it'll be a massacre."

Hatfield turned this over in his mind. Evidently the Ring A was ready, and would welcome the attack being arranged by outside forces. And they were not yet aware of General Simmons' murder.

When he awoke, he was fully refreshed. His back was stiff but better. He ate a hearty breakfast and sat on the corral fence, smoking. After a while John Hawk came out, one side of his face drawn up from the scabbed gash on his cheek, and a bandage bulking round his ribs.

"Hawk, meet Sonora Jim, the best shot I ever see," said Shorty.

The black eyes pierced the Ranger, who calmly returned the gaze. Hawk was of a suspicious nature and had a genius for spying. His blue-knuckled hands hung loose near the heavy guns, sagging in their holsters at his narrow waist.

"Saddle up," he grunted. "We're ridin'."

"All right."

Hatfield figured that the Hawk would try him out, of course, watch him for a time. The Hawk was a sneaking, sinister devil and with the terrific power of Marshall Aiken, they made a combination which Hatfield realized was close to unbeatable.

Saddling the golden sorrel, Hatfield fell into line as Aiken, John Hawk and two dozen gunnies rode away from the Ring A on a dirt trail, headed for the Pecos. He glimpsed the smoke of settler cabins now and again against the horizon, homes of subjects of Marshall Aiken.

As they rode, Hatfield kept alert, turning over in his mind what he had heard the previous night about the wiping out of the Girvinites.

"Got to learn more about that massacre business," he mused.

The wild Trans-Pecos land rolled up and down, cut by deep ravines choked with brush, bare mountain escarpments sticking to the blue sky. There was grass in plenty, and fat steers up all the draws, bearing ranch brands. There was great wealth here, but it was latent. It took time to gather, drive and market beeves, and the drain on the Emperor's exchequer must be immense. These gunnies were purely mercenary, in it for themselves, and would demand cash on the line to back Marshall Aiken.

Butterflies and birds flitted in the sunshine, and rattlesnakes lay in the shade under the berry bushes, waiting for victims, as the huge Aiken and the snaky Hawk led the procession. Shorty rode in the rear, keeping an eye on the recruit, Sonora Jim.

It was noon when they swung into a wide-mouthed valley, which narrowed and deepened as it dropped toward the Pecos. There was a Square G brand sign over the gate.

Swinging up to the single-storied, flat-roofed ranchhouse, Aiken and Hawk pulled up before the veranda. Hatfield saw the pretty golden-haired girl on the porch nod to the Emperor. He noted her youthful loveliness, the eager look Aiken gave her.

"Reckon this is the gal Purdue mentioned," he thought.

A stout, bulky man with bushy, graying hair, and a salted beard, limped out, leaning on a cane.

"Howdy, Aiken," he sang out. "Light and come in."

"Afternoon, Gillette," replied the Emperor, his attention on the girl.

This was the Square G. From Purdue's information, Hatfield knew this was where Len's brother had been staying when he had been drygulched. A couple of weeks had passed since the shootings, and the first awful pangs of grief had eased for the Gillettes.

The Ranger, with his long lashes shading his gray-green eyes, was taking everything in. He noted the lounging hands, sitting on the fence of the back corral. They wore black hats with Aiken's insignia. They greeted the Ring A gunnies like brothers.

"Aiken's got this place sewed up tight," he mused.

The shootings of Gillette's waddies had cut his forces in half, and Aiken had, on the pretense of helping the stricken father, put his own men here on the Square G.

The horses, lathered by the long run, were drinking from the troughs at the side of the house. Aiken and Hawk had gone into the front room with Peggy and her father. Jim Hatfield slouched in the shade of the low, rambling house. Nearby, the Ring A gunnies were talking, their speech larded with oaths. The smell of frying beef and boiling coffee came from the kitchen.

Windows were open and Hatfield edged toward one. He heard voices as he slouched in the shade against the wall.

"Look, Gillette," Aiken was saying in the nearby room, "I wanta pay back the eight thousand yuh lent me last week. I'm goin' to give yuh all the land south of yore present line to Wildcat Crik to wipe out the debt. Yuh must throw in the section north of yore valley rim, however. I need it, for it cuts me off from the Pecos that way."

"Why, Aiken," protested Gillette, "I got plenty range now — too much for what cows I own. Anyhow, I use that north section to run mustangs in. It's a natural pasture for hosses, and they can't stray far off."

"Huh," growled the Emperor. "Gillette, I been tryin' to help yuh out, 'count of yore losin' Phil. And I must say Peggy is the purtiest girl I ever see, and if she'll have me, why all she's got to do is say the word."

"That's up to her," replied Gillette. "I 'preciate yore tryin' to help me, Aiken. Bein' lame cramps me terrible. The men yuh sent over ain't worth a lick. They're lazy and don't like hard work. I'll have to hire me some new ones or the ranch'll go to pot."

"I'll send yuh some Mexes," promised Aiken. "I wish yuh'd see eye to eye with me on the trade, though. I ain't the sort to take no for an answer, Gillette. Not for long, anyways."

Hatfield heard the cold menace in the Emperor's voice. No doubt David Gillette caught it, too. Aiken, overbearing and too powerful to be thwarted by a single rancher, dominated his Pecos empire.

"Why's Aiken want that north section so bad?" wondered the listening Ranger. "He borrowed cash from Gillette, but only

76

enough to pay his gunnies for a few weeks. He'll need more pronto."

A short silence inside, then Gillette said, stubborn bitterness rising despite his crippled state:

" 'Pears to me yuh're puttin' the screws on me, Aiken. Yuh agreed on paper that north range is mine, and I've paid yore taxes and been neighborly with yuh for the sake of peace. Phil wanted to buck yuh. Mebbe he was right. We still got friends round the country."

"It don't pay to go agin me," snapped Aiken. "Yuh do what I tell yuh and yuh'll be a lot happier."

A knock on the closed door came, interrupting them.

"Dinner's ready," Peggy's clear voice announced.

"We'll finish this later, in a day or two," Aiken said quickly. The Emperor's voice softened, as he spoke to the girl. "Well, Miss Peggy, yuh're purtier than any pitcher ever painted."

They all went to the rear of the house to eat, and Hatfield drifted back to the bunkhouse where food was being served to the hands.

If Aiken made any further attempts to force Gillette to transfer to him the disputed north section of the Square G, the Ranger was unable to hear them. The emperor sat on the porch for a time, with Peggy, while John Hawk chatted with David Gillette, and young Frank practiced throwing a rope loop at a snubbing post.

At dark the Ring A outfit were back at the home ranch, Hatfield in the bunkhouse with many more gunnies. He wished he could learn the whole set-up, but knew he must move carefully.

Lights had been out in the bunkhouse for two hours when Hatfield started awake. A sixth sense gave him warning, and he came fully alert, hand stealing to a gun which lay close by him. Then, from outside, he heard the distant hooting of an owl, once, twice, a pause, then two short ones.

The door at the end of the long bunkhouse opened quietly, and a huge, dark shape bulked there came in.

Marshall Aiken, the Emperor of the Pecos, tiptoed over to John Hawk's bunk and bent down to shake his lieutenant. Hatfield, feigning sleep, heard the low voices.

"Hey, Hawk, rouse up!"

"What the hell's wrong?" demanded John Hawk.

"I just got the signal. The Guv'nor's waitin' for us. C'mon."

John Hawk rose hurriedly, strapped on his belt and guns, pulled on his boots and trailed Aiken outside.

"Huh," mused the Ranger, "this here Guv'nor must be somethin', routin' them two out at this time of night! Wonder if I can chance a peek?"

Snores of various calibres shook the building. Hatfield got up silently, put on boots, hat and guns, and stole to the door.

From the shadowed corner of the wall he saw Aiken and Hawk rapidly crossing an open stretch toward a stone springhouse near a rail fence which separated the main spread enclosure from a large pasture.

Just for life insurance, he located Goldy, grazing not far off in the big corral. He slapped his saddle on the sorrel, and led him outside the gate.

"Wait here, Goldy," he murmured.

Heading over toward the springhouse, he found he could not cut straight after Aiken and Hawk, since he would be exposed to easy view of the "Guv'nor", the owl-hooter so important that Hawk and the Emperor himself jumped to do his bidding.

He had to cross behind a stable, and slip around in front of the main house. Some tall oaks were on the north side of the house where he could conceal himself and approach quite near to the springhouse.

Chapter IX
Close Shave

Unable to guess what was occurring as he made these necessary moves, Jim Hatfield crept closer and closer, to hear what was said, and to identify the visitor.

Three shadowy figures stood on the far side of the stone hut. All the Ranger could make out were indistinct blobs in the darkness. One must be Aiken; another John Hawk. The third was muffled in a black cloak, his face turned from Hatfield, as inch by inch he sought to shift within earshot.

Had he been able to hear the Guv'nor's words, however, Hatfield would have known that death was at his heels.

"How are yuh, my boy?" the man in black asked the Emperor.

"Fine, fine," Aiken replied, his tone respectful. "What's up, that yuh come over tonight, Guv'nor?"

"You must get ready, pronto, Marshall. Now's the time to strike. You savvy the plan I worked out for you?"

"Shore, Guv'nor. We're ready any time yuh give the word."

"Good boy. Hawk, it's vital no slip be

made. Everything's arranged?"

"Yes, suh," growled John Hawk. "My men are set. We'll wipe out the whole damn crew."

"That'll finish it. There won't be any more strong fight against us. Not for a long while anyways."

"How about Simmons?" asked Aiken.

"General Simmons is dead."

"What!" exclaimed Aiken joyfully. "Who done it, Guv'nor?"

"Never mind. He's done for — that's the main thing. He was too damn clever for his own good, the old skunk. Now see here, I overheard somethin' mighty important, at Simmons'. There's a Texas Ranger operatin' in these parts, and he's across the Pecos right now, I reckon. Name's Hatfield, Jim Hatfield. Simmons called him Ranger, and yuh know the general sent word to Austin for help."

"A Ranger!" Aiken swore hotly.

"Damn his hide!" snarled Hawk. "What's this Ranger look like, Guv'nor?"

"He's over six feet, about Marshall's height, but not so beefy. Gray-green eyes, black hair, broad shoulders and slim waist. No whiskers. Watch his hands. They're slim, and he's fast as chain lightnin' —"

"My Gawd!" gasped Marshall Aiken. "It's him!"

"Who?" asked the Guv'nor.

"That new gunny I hired!"

"Yuh mean that Ranger Hatfield's right here on yore spread?" demanded the man in black harshly. "You fools, he'll learn everything!"

"He's here, all right," Hawk said grimly. "But he won't be for long."

"Kill him and be quick about it," ordered the Guv'nor. "Where is he now?"

"Snorin' in the bunkhouse," Aiken snapped.

"I hope yuh're right," the Guv'nor said dryly. "Go on — make sure of him. I believe he's the hombre that saved Purdue. He rode into Girvin a short while after Purdue escaped Hawk."

"Let's go," John Hawk ordered hoarsely, and drew a long bowie knife from his belt, its sharp blade glinting in the starlight. "I'll carve out his heart, damn him!"

The breed's Indian fury boiled. Aiken was in a killing mood, too.

"Wait a jiffy," commanded the Guv'nor. "The day'll be next Wednesday, so be set and ready."

"We'll be there," promised Aiken. "S'long, Guvnor, see yuh then."

"*Adios,* boy."

The Emperor of the Pecos and his terrible spy chief, John Hawk, started at high speed for the bunkhouse, murder in their hearts.

Pressed flat to the dirt at the base of a giant live-oak, its gnarled branches spreading a black cloak over him, Jim Hatfield froze as Marshall Aiken and Hawk suddenly hustled around the stone structure and headed for the bunkhouse.

"Now what's got 'em so excited?" he mused, ears wide.

A horse whinnied, back to the north, no doubt the mount belonging to the owl-hooter who had just had the conference with Aiken and Hawk. Hatfield placed the sound close to a tall black pine, where the rider must have left his horse before he climbed the fence into the Ring A yard.

Aiken and Hawk passed within twenty feet of Hatfield.

"That big jigger shore had me fooled!" he heard Hawk exclaim. "Lucky the Guv'nor warned us!"

"We gotta finish him pronto," growled Aiken. "One thing I hate is a Texas Ranger!"

They loped on toward the bunkhouse and Hatfield, warned now, started across the yard, meaning to fetch up at the horse corral and quietly get going before they discovered he was missing.

He glanced back at the springhouse, saw no one. The Guv'nor must be on his way. But he couldn't waste any seconds, and moved swiftly. A gun flashed from behind the springhouse, the bullet zipping within an inch of the Ranger.

He whirled, a long Colt jumping into his slim hand with the speed of magic, hammer spur back under thumb joint. He replied, chipping granite from the corner of the springhouse, spattering the face of his hidden foe.

Aiken and Hawk were at the bunkhouse, but at the sounds of shots they swung around and started his way.

Hatfield retreated swiftly for the front of the big ranchhouse, shooting as he ran, to prevent the man who had spied him from taking too careful aim.

"He's gone, Hawk!" he heard Marshall Aiken bellow.

John Hawk had started toward the flashes of Hatfield's gun, visible in the night.

"He's a spy, a Ranger spy!" the Hawk was shrieking. "Everybody out, boys! Hustle! Get Sonora Jim!"

Two hundred gunnies leaped to arms, crowding out of the long bunkhouse. Guns, pistols and rifles were snatched up, and the

84

fighting men hired by the Ring A rapidly went into action.

Hatfield, hidden by the bulk of the great ranchhouse, raised a shrill whistling. Both Colts filled and in his hands, he started away as the army of killers surged across the yard.

Their bullets were hunting him, blindly as yet, for he was still out of sight, except to the man behind the stone springhouse.

The Ranger saw the van of the gunnies coming around the house, and his Colts blasted them, his accurate aim unshaken by his peril.

He could hear leaden pellets whistling in the air, thudding in the ground around him, but it did not disturb his coolness. Three of the gunmen in front fell, bitten by his slugs, and he took shelter behind a thick tree trunk and began shooting in earnest.

The fury of the Ranger Colts stopped the charge. But only for moments.

"Go get him, damn yore hides!" he heard Hawk shrieking. "What yuh think yuh're paid for? Kill him!"

"Charge him, boys!" cried Aiken.

The shrill blasts of Hatfield's whistling punctuated the heavy gunfire. Down on one knee, bobbing out to rip them with bullets, the Texas Ranger appalled them by his terrific fighting power. Bunched as they were, he hardly needed to take aim to score hits. One bullet would tear through an arm or leg and strike a second gunny.

But a second gang came flying around another side of the great house, guns blazing in the darkness, war-whoops rising high. The first group started at him again, picking up momentum. He had to pause to throw fresh shells into his emptied revolvers.

"C'mon Goldy!" muttered the tall Ranger, as he prepared to sell his life dearly.

A shrill whinny rang out, and his pulses quickened. He put all his attention on killers coming around the house to divert them, for he saw Goldy galloping at full-tilt his way. The golden horse had heard Hatfield's call, but it had taken him precious minutes to come up, for he was too wary to approach close to the strange gunnies.

There were far too many of them for Hatfield to handle alone, and all he could hope for was to delay them for the time needed. He sang out to the big sorrel, whose tail and mane flew with the wind of his speed.

"This way, boy!" he roared.

Flashes, blue-yellow in the night, the constant explosions of heavy weapons, drifting clouds of powdersmoke, made the Ring

A spread a battlefield.

A slug kissed the Ranger's Stetson crown, passed through the felt. Another ricocheted on a rock and tore a hole in his sleeve, but did not damage him.

Goldy, unafraid of gunfire, knew how to handle himself in a scrap. The sorrel zigzagged as he moved, then suddenly turned and spurted over toward the big tree which was sheltering the Ranger.

Hatfield hastily pouched his Colts and seized the flying sorrel's mane in one hand and made Goldy's back, clinching his strong knees about the gelding's heaving ribs. Settling in his saddle, a prayer of thankfulness was in his heart that he had taken the precaution to slap leather on the sorrel and have him ready.

"Now run!" grunted the Ranger.

He pressed low over the golden horse's back, and Goldy dashed ahead. A guard was at the gates, waiting for them. Hatfield saw the dark figure, saw the glint of the rising pistol.

A dig in the ribs sent Goldy veering away. The Ranger whipped a Colt out and fired three quick ones that bowled the sentry head over heels, his revolver banging harmlessly in the air.

He put the sorrel straight at the fence, and

Goldy sailed high, cleared it, and landed on the other side.

Aiken saw the strategic error they had made. They had believed the Ranger would not be able to reach his horse.

"Get back and mount, pronto!" roared the Emperor. "A thousand dollars to the man who fetches in his scalp!"

A final burst of heavy gunfire finished the first phase of the attempt to kill Jim Hatfield, which he had prevented by his alert skill.

Swinging, the gunnies rushed for corrals to seize broncs. Some mounted bareback, not pausing to saddle up, but others slapped on hulls, cinched up, anticipating a long run, for the golden sorrel showed a speed almost incredible.

Hatfield had a good start and, keeping his Colts filled and ready, gave Goldy his head, riding along a dirt trail that ran sharply into the winding wagon road.

"Reckon we'll head for Girvin," he muttered, looking back over his shoulder.

The wind whistled shrilly past his ears with the flying sorrel's pace. Half a dozen of Hawk's gunnies swept from the open gate and roared after him.

In the night, shod hoofs struck fire from flinty rocks in the trail. Hatfield settled down to a steady gait.

"I wonder who that Guv'nor hombre can be!" he mused. "And how he savvies I'm a Ranger. Only place he could've learned that would've been by listenin' outside General Simmons' winder in Girvin. That moccasin track may give him away yet. 'Twas the same as the one where I picked up the bead!"

Such beads were usually strung on a piece of thread or hide strip. If broken, beads would keep working off.

The time for thought would come, but now he must put all his energy into shaking off the minions of the Emperor, urged on by Hawk.

A couple of faster mustangs, giving everything they had, drew up on Goldy. The Ranger was holding in a bit so the sorrel wouldn't run himself ragged. A bullet whistled too close for comfort to Hatfield's ear, and he swung, fired back a cylinder of slugs.

One of the two flew from his saddle as though snatched by a giant hand. The other, catching the ominous whine of lead about his head, slowed and dropped back among the bunch.

The range was too great for any of them to hope to hit him, save by a lucky shot.

They kept letting go with their Colts, but the tall Ranger's guns were respected by them, and none wished to draw up on him without full support.

For a perilous hour the golden sorrel's steady gallop kept on rhythmically. The pursuers were scattered along for a mile to the rear, but doggedly never let up.

"Reckon Aiken figgers on ridin' me down," muttered Hatfield. "Hmm, I'd like to git a fair crack at that Hawk snake!"

He needed time to cross the Pecos, could not afford to let them catch him in the water. Murderous hearts, filled with fury because of his triumphs over them, burned to see the finish of the Texas Ranger.

On and on, under the stars, the sorrel's hoofs slapping on the uneven road, galloped Jim Hatfield, running before the wrath of his foes.

A slip, a wrenched tendon in Goldy's leg, or a lucky pellet of lead would spell death. Death not only for the great Ranger, but for the brave men collected in Girvin by General Drew Simmons, who had given his life to the cause of justice and Texas.

Chapter X
Accusation and Confirmation

Len Purdue had been sorry to see his new friend leave Girvin. He watched the tall man disappear, then had gone and found a bite to eat. It was nearly morning; no use to return to bed.

He hung around until the sun bathed the plaza and the settlement buildings with yellow light.

The murder of General Drew Simmons was upon every man's tongue, and the fighters the old Texan had welded together into an army to force out the Emperor of the Pecos collected that morning to listen to Colonel Val Tydings and Mayor Abe Werner. Tydings was a fighting man, too, and proceeded to rally them.

Werner seemed in a bad humor, glum and silent. The finding of one of his coat buttons outside Simmons' window, while it hadn't directed much suspicion against the mayor, evidently troubled Werner himself. There was a fresh bruise, Purdue noted, on the bony-faced mayor's forehead.

"You know the general's plans, boys," Tydings told them grimly. "He wouldn't want us to quit. Aiken must be made to pay for all the wrongs he's done us."

Len Purdue lounged around, ready to start for the Ring A and fight when the word came. They needed more arms and ammunition, and good strategy to take such a big gang in its stronghold.

While Colonel Tydings was busy, talking with some of his lieutenants, the big, bearded Dan Chock, who had been a friend of Drew Simmons and active the night before when they had accused Jim Hatfield of the killing, came hustling up. He was dragging a small, shrinking man with a cherry-red nose and pale hair.

"Hey, Colonel!" Chock bawled excitedly. "Listen to what Rabbit has to say!"

"Rabbit" Withers was one of the town loafers. Now and then he worked in the grocery store, but usually was to be found bumming drinks at the saloons. He had a weak chin and a sharp nose. Greenish eyes blinked nervously as the heavy-handed Chock literally heaved him through the air and held him up before Tydings.

Rabbit's teeth chattered violently as the colonel frowned upon him sternly. His clothes were old and dirty. Corduroy pants were tucked into worn boots, and he wore a ragged blue shirt and straw hat discarded by its former owner.

"Aw, cut it out, Dan," begged Rabbit Withers. "I dunno nothin'."

"Yes, yuh do," insisted Chock, shaking him. "Tell the colonel what yuh told me when I bought yuh a drink jest now. C'mon, talk! Pronto!" He shook Rabbit until the little man's bones rattled.

"Hurry, Withers, if you've anything to tell me," commanded Colonel Val Tydings. "I'm a busy man this morning."

Rabbit blinked, licked his lips apprehensively.

"He — he'll kill me," he whined. "I'm scared."

"You needn't be," Tydings replied. "We'll protect you, Rabbit."

Rabbit gulped. The forceful Chock had him in an iron grip, and the colonel's strong eyes bored to his shrinking soul.

"Don't let him get me, now," he quavered. "Yuh promised."

"Yes, yes. What is it?"

"Well — yuh shore yuh won't let him kill me if I tell? Well, I — I — I was in my shack — that's behind the general's, yuh savvy — last night."

"Full of red-eye, as usual," a citizen interpolated, and a chuckle ran through the crowd.

"Mebbe," admitted Rabbit Withers. "Jest the same I could hear, and I could see, too." He blinked apprehensive eyes over the gathering, and seemed reassured. "I heard shots and yells, and I gets up and peeks out, careful-like of course, so's not to draw no lead. I see a man standing outside the general's back winder, a-shootin' and stompin' there."

Abe Werner suddenly livened up.

"What'd this man look like, Rabbit?"

"He was one great big feller. I seen him against the lighted winder, though right soon out goes the lamp. He runs hell-for-leather up Tin Can Alley, then comes a-howlin' back, and — well, I reckon I had enough red-eye in me to perk me up, for I drawed my pistol and shot one at him."

"You?" demanded Tydings unbelievingly. "You fired at the assassin?"

"Yes, suh. I wouldn't have if I'd been sober, but I'd had plenty. I think I hit him, too, in the back, for he throws up his head like a busted cayuse and nearly goes down. Then he jumps up and runs toward the street, and Dan Chock rushes in with you folks."

"H'm," growled Tydings, his face stern. "A strange story, Rabbit. Why didn't you tell us this last night, while we were investigating?"

Rabbit Withers shrugged. "I made up my mind to keep shut," he answered sullenly. "I didn't like that big jigger's looks a-tall, and I still feel the same. But wantin' a drink mighty bad, I done told some of it to Dan and he drug me over here."

"You should have come forward at once, Withers," Tydings snapped severely. "You're a fool."

"Yes, suh. I reckon I am."

Len Purdue's head swam, as he realized the full import of Rabbit Withers' confession. Although Jim Hastings — as he knew the man who had snatched him from death — had made a deep impression upon him, this fresh evidence turned suspicion instantly upon the stranger.

"Could yuh point out the hombre yuh took a shot at?" Werner asked.

Withers nodded. "Yeah, 'cause I kept on peekin' and seen all that happened later. You fellers come along, and the colonel, too, and I heard yuh threatenin' to lynch that big jigger. But he talked yuh outa it somehow, for he was let go."

Dumfounded silence fell upon the men of Girvin. That tall fellow who had been creased across the back muscles had made fools of them. He had shot General Drew

Simmons, had run out, fired some bullets through the window, and had feigned to be pursuing the killer and —

"Where's that Hastings?" cried Tydings, and the demand was echoed through the crowd.

Len Purdue, who had lied to save his friend, was flabbergasted. As they recalled what he had told them, accusing looks, filled with suspicion, were cast at the tall young waddy.

"Mebbe I was wrong, boys," muttered Purdue. "I was shore I saw a rider hittin' off. Jim Hastin's left town this mornin', before it was light. Killers come to my shack and tried to finish us off, as you know, and Hastings hit outa town. Yuh can't think I'm guilty of anything wrong, or I would've gone with him."

"Yeah, yuh're okay, Purdue," Chock finally growled. "It's that jigger. He fooled smarter folks than me'n you."

"His runnin' away cinches it," declared "Slim" Orville, tall and lean, with lantern jaw and bald dome.

"He must be a spy for Marshall Aiken!" cried Abe Werner. "An underhand, night-crawlin' drygulcher who killed the gen'ral and tried to lay it on me by droppin' that button! And if yuh ask me, he ain't far away from Girvin right now."

"What makes you think so?" demanded Colonel Tydings.

"Huh! See this bump on my head? I kept quiet about it, but I took it last night. Couldn't sleep, thinkin' of what'd happened, and somebody tried to creep up on me and do me in. I got this wound when I run out and hit the edge of the door. But when I meet him, I'll savvy him, damn his hide."

"How so?"

Werner shrugged. "I got an idea," he said cryptically.

Len Purdue still couldn't believe it.

"But if he is an Aiken man, Colonel, why'd he keep 'em from killin' me?"

Val Tydings lifted an eyebrow. "I don't know, unless it was a clever trick to use you later on for something more important, Purdue."

Sadly Len stuck around, trying to figure it out. He kept thinking of Peggy Gillette, hungered for another sight of her.

"But Aiken has the inside track," he mourned unhappily.

That night he rode to thick chaparral south of Girvin, rolled in his blanket under the stars.

"Why did Jim save me?" he kept asking

97

himself, over and over. It was a muddle to him.

With the fresh, aromatic air of morning in his lungs, Len Purdue came to a decision.

"We'll go over there," he told the black mare, "and I'll tell her all there is to know about Aiken. She oughta savvy about her brother and mine and everything. I can't believe she'd cotton to such a man."

He had been eating his heart out to see Peggy, ever since he had been run off the Square G, though he tried to make himself believe that his only purpose for staying in the Pecos country now was to clear up the murder of his brother and Peggy Gillette's brother Phillip. That was of vital importance, of course — but so was Peggy.

He saddled up the black mare, and rode determinedly to the crossing.

But once over the Pecos wild canyon, Purdue rode with caution. Once an old-timer had shown him how to proceed in hostile country, hiding his own trail as far as he could, and making sure he wasn't being followed, and he was following those instructions now.

He found a deer track that ran close to the Pecos, and kept on that instead of the main way, where he might bump into the minions of Marshall Aiken.

It was afternoon when he came upon the valley in which stood the Square G ranchhouse. As the stream which ran through it approached its confluence with the sombre Pecos, the valley narrowed to a canyon which blocked further progress in that direction.

Swinging around, he began picking a slow route through dense bush lining the ravine, and after a couple of miles, he could see, off in the distance, the buildings of the Gillette ranch.

Keen eyes narrowed against the brilliant sunlight, he stared down at the home of the girl he had fallen in love with, and who, unhappily for Len Purdue, was desired by Marshall Aiken, Emperor of the Pecos.

Coming up closer, Purdue saw horsemen riding down the valley toward the ranch. He dismounted and, going out on a red bluff, lay flat and watched.

"That's Aiken," he growled, and anger flared hot in his heart.

He saw the sinister Hawk, too, and then his eyes traveled through the gunny band. A figure he knew made him gasp. It was Jim Hastings!

"Yeah, he's ridin' for Aiken," growled Purdue. "I got to believe it now!"

Rabbit Withers' story was confirmed, and

Purdue was stricken with a sickening misery.

He lay up there, watching. It was an hour before Aiken and Hawk emerged and, mounting, rode away with their fighting men, Jim among them.

But from his eyrie young Purdue could see figures around the Square G, in black hats. They were hands placed there by Aiken, and he couldn't walk into their clutches.

"Sooner or later," he thought, "she'll come out, where I can talk to her alone."

However, the dark came without him seeing Peggy Gillette, and Len Purdue slept through the night, camped in the bush, back from the valley rim.

CHAPTER XI
CAPTURE

Broad daylight had come when Purdue woke up, and someone was whistling not far away. On the alert for enemies, he arose and tiptoed toward the sound.

He caught sight of a man bending down among upheaved rocks, thickly overgrown with brush. Through a vista in the chaparral, Purdue observed him.

Creeping closer, he saw the man straighten, and when he turned around,

Purdue recognized Frank Gillette, Peggy's kid brother. The youth's Stetson was shoved back on his brown-haired head, and he whistled with the carefree abandon of youth.

"What's he got in his hand?" muttered Len, catching the shine of something Frank had picked up from the thick grass and was turning over and over in his palm.

Purdue had liked Frank, and was sure he could trust him. Frank's saddled horse stood back a distance from the young fellow. The mount scented Purdue's mare and whinnied. Frank swung around. Len rose up.

"Howdy, Frank," he said.

Young Gillette started, but grinned as he recognized Purdue.

"Yuh snuk up on me," he remarked.

"What yuh got there?" asked Purdue.

"It's a busted watch. I picked it up close to the cave entrance."

"There's a cave in there?"

"Shore. I been in it, but not lately. There's signs somebody's been around, though."

Purdue stretched his neck to look at the big silver watch which Frank had found. One edge was out of shape, and the crystal was cracked. He gasped with stunned surprise. He knew that timepiece!

"Gimme it," he cried. "That was my

dad's, Frank!"

"Yore dad's? What was he doin' here?"

"He wasn't here. But my brother Harry always toted it, after dad died. Lookit the initials, 'HCP.' "

Purdue turned the watch over and over. His mouth worked and cold sweat came out on his brow, as the full force of this remembrance of his elder brother hit him.

"Harry musta dropped it," said Frank.

"Huh! It was shot outa his pocket, I'd say. Where was his body found?"

"Oh, couple miles north of here, along with Phil's."

"They were shot here, and toted off," growled Purdue. "The bullet tore through Harry's back, knocked the watch out. Let's look around."

There were footprints in softer spots, but much sign had been effaced. However, Purdue found a chunk of lead he figured was from a rifle, plastered on a protruding rock near the spot where Frank had picked up the watch.

"Ain't no doubt Harry was shot while he was stoopin' over," growled Purdue. "They got yore brother at the same time."

"It's all mighty queer. This is our range, and why anybody'd wanta kill pore Phil, I dunno. Aiken says it was men from Girvin."

"Aiken's a damn' liar!"

Purdue took in some scratches and digs on the rocks, while Frank pointed out the black entry to the cave. The hole was not large, but when Purdue crawled through he found that the chamber widened. He struck matches, but after a time he and Frank found themselves blocked by a pile of rocks, and turned back to the sunlight.

"Don't let Aiken and Hawk know I been around, Frank," Purdue cautioned. "They're gunnin' for me. I reckon Aiken's got men at yore house, ain't he?"

"Yeah, helpin' us out, but they're a lazy crew. Good for nothin'."

"I'm mighty anxious to talk to yore sister. Yuh s'pose if I waited down the valley trail, yuh could get her to come out and see me?"

"I guess so. C'mon."

An hour later Purdue rose up from his place of concealment, and Peggy Gillette, her face pale and filled with trouble, dismounted from her white horse.

"Why are you here?" she asked quickly. "You shouldn't have come. It's too dangerous."

"I had to see yuh," he said humbly.

The girl was nervous, as she looked into the tall young waddy's eyes. The scent of the wildflowers and chaparral was sweet on the morning breeze, the chirp of birds in their ears.

"Miss Peggy," Len said, "I can't put yuh outa my mind. That's the honest truth."

He didn't know how it happened — nor did she. But the next instant he had suddenly gathered her in his arms and was kissing her. For a moment while the world stood still, her warm lips returned his kiss. Then she pushed him away.

"You mustn't ever do that again," she said firmly. "Never, do you hear?"

"But I love yuh, Peggy! I love yuh, I tell yuh —"

She began to sob, face in her hands, and Purdue was all contrition. The metallic click of a cocking gun brought him to a sudden realization of danger.

"Throw up yore paws!" a cold voice snapped.

John Hawk, a wraith gliding through the chaparral, was right behind Purdue, a rifle held short and ready in his bony hands.

Somebody else came running up, and the pinned waddy saw it was Marshall Aiken, Emperor of the Pecos.

"Yuh got him, Hawk?" cried Aiken.

"Not the one we're after," growled Hawk, "but he'll do, Boss." A fierce glow came into the breed's flat-black eyes. "I know'd I'd take yuh, agin, Purdue. This time yuh won't get away."

"Peggy," bawled Aiken. "What yuh doin' up here with this crowbait?"

Red death was upon Purdue, captive of the Emperor of the Pecos. . . .

The golden sorrel did not fail Jim Hatfield, did not make that slip which would have spelled violent death to the Texas Ranger who was bucking the all-powerful legions of Marshall Aiken, Emperor of the Pecos.

Goldy sped on, warm lather coming out on his buckskin hide, mane and tail swishing in the wind as they led the Ring A gunnies a mad chase.

Dust beat into the night air, drummed up by hundreds of hoofs. Shots, the red flashes of the explosions, and war-whoops threatening what would happen when the furious Ring A came up with their arch-enemy, mingled in a horrid din.

Coolly the Ranger rode, keeping them at a respectful distance with his mighty Colts. He would tire them, then elude them.

"Reckon they'll figger I'm headin' straight to Girvin crossin'," he mused, "so they'll ride there even if I leave 'em behind."

He needed darkness in which to shake them off, so low over Goldy, he crooned words of encouragement.

"Show 'em what runnin' means, boy," he told the sorrel, and with a snort, the great horse added another drive to his pace and began pulling away.

Spurs were being cruelly gouged into sweated mustang flanks behind the Ranger, quirts tattooing hides, as Hawk and Aiken roared to their gunmen to stay up with the man out front.

But it was impossible. Inexorably Goldy gained yard after yard, and the horsemen behind, stringing out again, howled with baffled anger as they saw the gelding leaving them, growing indistinct in the dimness.

Swinging a wide curve, the Ranger glanced back. The van was still in the distance. Hatfield jerked his right rein, and Goldy veered. Hatfield's tall body leaned far to the side as they made the turn onto a narrow side trail.

"It'll take 'em a few minutes to figger that out, and some of 'em'll stick on the road," he informed the sorrel, his companion on so many missions.

Pushing south, he swung off the trail, and took to another of the narrow deer trails. Enveloped in high mesquite, with thorns brushing leather and hide, he allowed Goldy to ease down and regain his wind, for it had been a terrific gallop.

Guns freshly loaded and holstered, the Ranger kept his ears open for sounds of pursuit. Aiken and John Hawk would not give up.

In front of him as he neared the Pecos, impassable save at certain fords, he saw a streak of lighter sky on the horizon, presaging the new day. Soon it would be easier to spot a fugitive, even though hidden in the chaparral. Keen eyes from high points might note the winging away of birds from a horseman's path, or rising dust, even the glint of sun scintillating on metal accoutrements.

As the light grew, it found the tall Ranger, dust-covered, with chin strap tight under his grim jaw, pushing up along a ridge that swung over toward the Pecos.

"Must be nearin' that Square G setup, where Purdue's girl lives," he muttered, eyes sweeping the valley.

He started, turned in his saddle as he reined in the sorrel, for he caught a sign of dust rising in the forested gap to one side.

"Huh! They've short-cut me. Must be headin' for the ford below. That'll be the Hawk. He's got too much Injun in him to be fooled for long!"

He looked behind, and from that direction, though farther off, dust also was visible.

"Tryin' to pocket us," he told Goldy.

Back in the mesquite on the ridge, he could glimpse speeding horsemen, quirting and spurring full-tilt.

"I savvy! If they cover the Square G, they'll have me! That barranca'll cut me off."

He calculated the chances of beating them to the pass, but shook his head.

"Quicker me'n Hawk have a settlin'," he thought, "the easier it'll be! That breed's too all-fired smart, and he savvies these trails better'n I do!"

Hidden from below, in case they should look his way, he lost sight of Hawk, Aiken and the score of gunnies accompanying them, as they swung in the direction of the Gillettes' Square G ranch.

The sun was reddening the eastern horizon as the tall Ranger hunted back with his slitted, gray-green eyes. Black specks winged up in the sky, and he watched, knowing them to be crows. By their movements he could follow the progress of riders, split off from the bunch slowly approaching his position. They had picked up his direct trail and, now that it was light, could move faster.

He was stopped from further progress

toward the fords unless he chose to expose himself and start the run again. He might head west, but he did not fancy a long, useless, roundabout ride that might occupy a couple of days. He was in a hurry to reach Girvin and rally the fighting men there.

He pivoted Goldy and cut for the point where he had noted the split of the northern bunch, and rode rapidly at an angle to the approaching gunnies. Not yet had they seen him, but they would pick up his sign.

It was tough going in spots, but he pushed the golden gelding relentlessly on, finally coming on a narrow path that wound for the Pecos. It was little used, overgrown with thorned bush, but freshly broken branches showed that men had just come through. He could read that from indentations in softer spots, too.

"Must be a way over here," he deduced.

He whispered to the sorrel, patting the arched neck, and as they neared the river, Goldy gave him warning, softly sniffing, rippling his hide.

Jim Hatfield dismounted, led the horse into the bush, and with his rifle in his hands, stole toward the deep canyon.

The whiff of cigarette smoke came to his sensitive nostrils. Crouching low, he edged in, and saw four horses, bleeding from spur and quirt marks, heavily lathered, standing with drooped heads, reins on the ground. As the Ranger crept on, he heard a low murmur of voices.

Through a narrow gap in the chaparral, he recognized Shorty, one of the Ring A lieutenants, his vicious face set as he drew on a brown-paper cigarette, squatted with his bowlegs under him. Three gunnies were in the group with Shorty, covering this approach to the river.

"The big skunk ain't likely to head this-a-way," he heard Shorty growl to the others. "He's gone further south. They'll pick him up near the Square G shore."

CHAPTER XII
RANGER ALONE

Quickly Hatfield's rifle came up to the shoulder. Speed was essential, for he needed the start to make the dangerous crossing of the Pecos. The canyon was just ahead, and he could see the steplike path dropping into it. A horse could get down there, if properly led, and he could hear the purring of the rapids funneling up from the rocky walls.

The cluck-cluck of the cocking carbine was followed by the steely voice of the Ranger.

"Rise up, gents, and unbuckle yore gun-belts!"

With a violent start, the four realized their quarry was upon them. The hunted had become the hunter, and they were trapped. Two quickly reached, but Shorty and the man between the bowlegged devil and Hatfield elected to fight it out.

Hatfield's rifle exploded with a whiplike snap. Shorty's mate, his Colt half up, threw back his head. His pistol went off, but the slug burrowed into the earth. As he crashed, the breath of time gave Shorty his chance. The bowlegged lieutenant of the Ring A snapped a bullet at Hatfield with terrific speed, guessing his position by the Winchester's sound. The leaden pellet tore a chunk from the Ranger's Stetson crown.

Before Shorty could let go again, however, the carbine swung and cut him down. His arm relaxed, his knees buckled, and a blue spot showed between the hard, vicious eyes. Bowlegs no longer holding him up, Shorty folded beside the corpse of his pard.

"Don't — don't shoot!" gasped a third man. "We quit!"

His partner's teeth were chattering as he tried to beg off, too.

Leaping to his feet, the Ranger, eyes cold as ice, leaped toward them, carbine held short in his hands, finger through the trigger guard.

He knew that the shooting would be heard by other hunting parties, that they would converge swiftly upon the spot.

"Unbuckle and drop, I said!" he snarled.

Scared eyes blinked as they obeyed, always watching the grim face of the big fighting man. Their heavy belts, loops shining with .45 shells and holsters full of guns, dropped around their booted feet, and they stepped away at the Ranger's command.

He whistled, and Goldy came trotting up to him.

"Get goin'!" he snapped. "Pronto! Lead my hoss down to the river."

One seized the sorrel's reins, and slid over the brink. The other followed, while the tall man came last, covering them with his steady weapon.

It was a difficult descent, down along narrow rock ledges where the sorrel's footing was precarious, but at last Goldy stood hock-deep in the Pecos.

"Swim across," Hatfield ordered. "I'll kill yuh if yuh try any tricks."

"But, mister, we'll likely drown in them rapids below, without a hoss to help us!" wailed one.

"Dry up!"

Hatfield forced them into the water at carbine point, and they waded out, began to swim, while the Ranger mounted and started the sorrel over. With the strong horse, he could make better time and not be carried down so far, and he hit the opposite bank while the gunnies were still in the water, near the rock-crusted rapids.

They just managed to make it, clinging to a rock above the narrowing of the canyon like drowned rats, as he led the sorrel up the steep bank.

He reached the top in the nick of time. Shouts and shots sounded from across the deep canyon, and as he rode off a whole gang of the Hawk's gunnies were coming hell-for-leather along the trail.

With a laugh, he spurred full-tilt away, for Girvin town. . . .

The sun was yellow and hot as he came to the outskirts of the settlement. He could see the alleys, piled with tin cans that had been thrown out back doors, and mongrel dogs, chickens and pigs. Children were playing, and along Main Street a number of men were visible on the plaza.

Jim Hatfield slowed Goldy, walking the sorrel between the scattered houses toward the center of the town. A man on a chestnut horse rode out from between two cabins, and pulled up short as he saw the tall Ranger.

It was Dan Chock, the big, bearded man.

"Howdy, Chock," Hatfield called.

To his amazement, Chock uttered a warwhoop and dug for his Colt. He was in his saddle, and luckily the chestnut jumped at the rider's yell, so that Chock's bullet whirled wide of Hatfield, singing like a giant wasp past his ear.

"Yuh fool, hold it!" roared Hatfield.

"Hey, Colonel Tydings — Mayor Werner! Here he is!" bellowed Dan Chock, and sought to control the pirouetting horse so he could kill the tall man. "C'mon boy, take him!"

His pistol flashing out, his lips straight in a grim line, Hatfield drove Goldy in, covering the yards between Chock and himself in a jiffy. Chock, however, had managed to get control over his mount and again was taking aim at Hatfield, who saw the red light of death in the husky citizen's fierce eyes.

He had to fire, and quickly, to save himself. Chock's face was blazing red, his black beard bristling in fury at sight of the tall Texas Ranger.

Hatfield's big Colt roared. Chock's gun flew from his hand, and he let out a yelp of anguish. His fingers were cut and stung, and he shook his paining arm, while the chestnut reared on his hind legs, snorting and squealing in terror.

Hatfield grabbed at the giant citizen's reins, jerked down the chestnut's head.

"I didn't want to hurt yuh, Chock," he said quickly. "Why did yuh fire on me?"

"Yuh can't scare me!" shrieked Chock. "Go on and shoot! Yuh dirty killer, we're onto yore tricks! Yuh killed the general! Rabbit Withers seen yuh do it! Everybody's out to get yore hide, and the colonel'll see to it yuh're took!"

"Yuh're loco! I told yuh I didn't shoot Simmons. He was a friend of mine. Where's Purdue? He'll tell yuh —"

"Purdue's left! He won't back yuh no more!" Chock cursed him furiously.

Deep creases between his gray-green eyes, Hatfield looked toward the plaza. Men had heard the shooting, and Chock's yells, and were already starting his way, grabbing up rifles and Colts.

"The fools," muttered the Ranger.

For some reason the town had turned violently against him. The very people he sought to assist were bent on killing him.

He knew the wild hearts of such men. They would shoot first and ask questions later. They were sure of his guilt now.

115

"Rabbit Withers spotted yuh," shouted Chock, "and yuh was seen ridin' with Aiken's gang!"

Bullets began singing over Hatfield's head, though with Chock so close they couldn't blast him straight without endangering Dan. Some came on foot, others leaped on horses, spurring down the plaza.

Hatfield had only a breath in which to figure.

He had not expected this sort of welcome.

"Now listen, Chock —" he began.

But Dan Chock, as Hatfield had glanced away from him, had thought he saw his chance. The big man knocked up the Ranger's right arm with a quick flip of his uninjured hand, and threw both arms around Hatfield, half dragging the Texas Ranger from his leather.

"I got him, boys!" shrieked Chock. "He'll stretch hemp this mornin'!"

Hatfield's knees pressed the sorrel, and Goldy jerked back and away. The sudden, unexpected move dragged Chock off the chestnut, and the swinging of the Ranger's body wrenched his right arm free as Chock hung on, seeking to pull him to earth.

The van of the citizens was coming hell-for-leather. He had to act fast, so cracked his Colt barrel hard on Chock's head.

Chock's grip relaxed, and he slid down, bounced off the leather-tapped stirrup. He hit dust, lying quiet.

Whirling, Hatfield rode out of Girvin, while bullets whistled about him, snapping at his Stetson and leather. Whoops of anger punctuated the din, and the dry dust rose up into clouds.

Pandemonium reigned in Girvin while Hatfield, aware they would fill him full of lead before they would listen to him, galloped away. He doubted if they would now believe he was a Ranger.

For miles they followed, spending their energy in an effort to overtake the golden sorrel. A dozen, on fast horses, doggedly kept running after him, with Girvin far behind. They clung to his trail, shooting whenever they came within range.

It was not until the sun dropped behind the blue mountains across the Pecos that this citizen band gave up, and the fagged sorrel, dust-coated and wet, could slow and manage to regain some wind.

"Looks like we're all alone, Goldy," the Ranger muttered, wiping alkali from his eyes.

The thing to do was sleep, and Hatfield unsaddled the sorrel and let him roll.

A spring furnished water, and the Ranger

wrapped in his blanket to forget it all in much needed rest.

Chapter XIII
A Nice Find

The first streak of the new day fetched Jim Hatfield awake. Refreshed, he pulled on his boots. Getting his cake of soap from his saddlebag, he made a lather and scraped the beard stubble from his face, spruced up, becoming his trim self once more. His back was stiff, but outside of that he felt fine.

Goldy came at his call, and after grooming and watering the sorrel, the Ranger mounted and started for the Pecos. He was again heading alone for Marshall Aiken's empire.

"Have to keep up with their plans," he told Goldy. "That there massacre they spoke of'll soon be set. If I can settle things with Hawk, that'll be a step in the right direction."

The Guv'nor, he figured, was a clever devil, even more so than Aiken and the Hawk. Behind them the vague, terrible figure seemed to plan horror after horror, to spy out Hatfield's moves, to destroy the mounting opposition to the Emperor. Simmons had been murdered, attempts made on the Ranger, on Werner, on Purdue.

"I'll get him!" he muttered.

He was far south and, locating a crossing, reached the wilds west of the deep canyon of the Pecos. It took most of the morning to ride up and make up the distance lost in eluding the blindly infuriated Girvinites. Then he recognized a landmark, and knew he was in the vicinity of the Square G.

And suddenly he heard a woman crying. He pulled the sorrel to a halt.

She was sobbing as though her heart would break. Hatfield, troubled at this distress, dismounted. Pushing up a rise in the woods, he spied Peggy Gillette.

She was sitting on a fallen log, and her white horse waited nearby. Her face was in her hands, and her small, dainty figure was hunched over. Sobs were shaking her.

"Hey, Sis, Sis!"

A call rang out in a high-pitched, boyish voice.

The Ranger drew back. Peggy Gillette quickly dried her tears and arose, smiling as her brother Frank came riding up and jumped off his mustang.

"They got Purdue at the Ring A, all right, Sis," reported Frank. "They're keepin' him locked in a shack behind the smokehouse, and they ain't hurt him much."

"I'd hate to think Marshall would injure anyone," the girl replied gently.

"What yuh been cryin' for?" asked Frank.

"Oh, nothing. I turned my ankle, that's all."

"Yuh mean to marry up with Marshall day after tomorrer, Sis?" asked Frank earnestly, trying to hold her gaze.

"Certainly. Wednesday night. I gave my promise. Why, Frank?"

Frank shrugged, and looked down at his booted feet.

"I dunno. Only Dad said if yuh didn't love Aiken, why that was yore affair. Yuh know, I believe that Purdue feller sorta liked yuh, Sis. But Aiken says Purdue shot and killed one of his men, and I reckon Purdue's harder'n he seems. Jest the same, it's a puzzle 'bout that watch of Purdue's brother's."

"What watch?" she asked, preoccupied with her thoughts.

"The one we picked up at the cave north of the ranch. Purdue figgered Harry and Phil was killed there, and then their bodies dumped where they was found. Reckon I'll ride up there agin. Wanta come and see?"

"No, Frank, I'm going back to Dad. He needs me."

She mounted her white horse, and brother

120

and sister rode off. Hatfield returned to Goldy, trailing after them.

"So they got Purdue again," he thought. "Why ain't they killed him?"

And why, he wondered, had the two murdered men been shifted?

"Must be a good reason for movin' corpses," he decided. "I'll have to have a look-see at that cave. Aiken and Hawk most likely drygulched 'em."

Later in the day, from a screen of brush, he watched Frank Gillette fooling around the cavern mouth, but Frank soon mounted and rode back home.

Hatfield approached, and began poking about the place. Making sure no one was at hand, he ducked inside and proceeded till he came to the pile of rocks that had stopped Purdue.

He began pulling these down, and after a half hour's hard work, had made a hole large enough to crawl through. The cavern, he saw as he struck a match, widened out. A burlap bag on a flat rock attracted him. It held several sticks of dynamite in it, fuses and caps.

"Huh! Jest what I want! If I can catch Aiken and his gunnies in that barranca below that dam, I'll wash some of the fight out of 'em."

He had meant to get explosives in Girvin, but had been chased by the army he sought to help. Now he had dynamite, and it fitted in with a clever plan he had made.

He spent some time examining the interior walls of the cavern, after which he eased out, blocked up the hole, and with the bag in one hand, emerged into the late, warm afternoon sunlight.

"If they've taken Purdue," he mused, "then I'll have to rescue him again. Aiken and the Hawk'll kill him. It's a wonder they didn't string him right off! Wonder if that gal kept 'em from it?"

Hatfield dried out the caps, fuses and sticks of dynamite by laying them on a flat rock in the sun. Then he carefully wrapped them and stowed them in the warbag at his cantle. Mounting, he rode to a high point, looked around the country for signs of enemies. The coast was clear, so he started for the Ring A, expecting to approach the big spread in the darkness and see about snatching Purdue from their hands.

Hatfield spent the rest of the daylight in crossing toward Aiken's spread. He could not travel on any main trail, for he knew they would be watching them. At last he found himself nearing the great reservoir he had noted during his first trip in here. The drainage stream from the high stone dam ran through its narrow, deep canyon, with a good trail at the bottom that wound in and out as the water ran toward its meeting with the Pecos.

"Wouldn't be a bad way to come up on the spread," he thought. "An army could travel through that gap in daytime and never be seen, 'less someone looked right down from the rims!"

And yet, as he had already thought, it would be a perfect place for an ambush to catch men in the constricted barranca.

Crossing these deep gashes in the surface was a job, unless one was acquainted with the terrain. He had come over here before, so knew that below the banks widened so that it was possible to get up or down.

It was after midnight when he left the sorrel back in the mesquite and stole toward the buildings of the Ring A. To his surprise, lights blazed in them, and he could see many men moving about. The clang of blacksmith hammers told him that horses were being shod, and steel worked.

He glanced toward the smokehouse. In the small hut behind it, where bars were nailed over the one window and the door padlocked, they were holding Len Purdue. It was in plain sight of the busy gunnies, and he could never get in and take Purdue out under such circumstances.

For an hour the Ranger waited, thinking they would calm down and turn in. Instead, they had some coffee and food, and around two in the morning they saddled up. Nearly two hundred fighting men, heavily armed with rifles, shotguns and pistols, and led by John Hawk, rode out of the Ring A and took the trail.

Flat on his belly in a dense thicket, the Ranger saw the glint of fierce eyes, bristling mustaches and beards, the gun-girdled torsos of the killers. Where were they heading?

He was worried, for why should such a gang ride the night trails? He heard the creak of leather, the clopping of many hoofs, and the rough jests of the men.

"This is goin' to be real sport, Nevada!" one sang out to a pard.

"We'll wipe out the skunks, every one of 'em!" called back the gunny addressed.

John Hawk, too, overheard, and the lean breed swung swiftly around in his saddle.

"Quiet, back there," he called back. "Yuh wanta warn everybody? Keep yore lips buttoned, yuh fools."

Marshall Aiken rode with a bodyguard of six big gunmen.

When they had all passed his vantage point, Hatfield crept back to the sorrel, mounted, and rode up near the stone springhouse where he had glimpsed the muffled, cloaked Guv'nor the night they had discovered his identity and sought to slay him.

"Now's the chance to git Purdue, but it'll hafta be fast," he muttered, searching the ranch with his keen eyes. "I can't lose sight of that gang!"

For he deducted they were riding to that "massacre" of which he had heard before — the massacre of Colonel Val Tydings and his men!

The first thing he did, after leaving Goldy hidden, was to take his lariat and rope a bronc from the great enclosed pasture. Rope bridles were hanging handy on the top rail, and he slid one over the animal's head, leaving him handily tethered.

The Ring A had quieted down, and he could see no men moving. Lights were out, save for a lamp that burned in the big house. However, as he went through the fence and scuttled in the dense shadows, he caught the red glow of a cigarette at the front of Len Purdue's prison hut.

A guard was sitting there, shoulders to the log wall.

Hatfield crept to the back of the small shack, and around it until he could, as he crouched frozen, almost hear the breathing of the sentry.

He tensed for a spring. Just as he jumped, long Colt barrel up, the gunny happened to turn and look full at him.

"Hey!"

With a rising yell, the guard sought to grab up his rifle. The Ranger landed, and the gunny grunted as he was knocked flat, though he managed to duck the full force of the descending steel cylinder.

"Help! Help!"

The shrill cry rang out, and the Texas Ranger cursed, knowing it would bring the home gang upon him within a minute. He got his man by the throat, and banged his head against the bottom log, swiftly disposing of him. Leaping to his feet, he threw a mighty shoulder against the stout oak door. He burst it in, but the padlock chain held.

"Purdue!" he cried.

To his relief, the waddy replied.

"Yeah? Who is it?"

"It's Jim! I'm takin' yuh out, pronto! Look out, I'm goin' to shoot the lock off."

He placed his Colt muzzle close to the big padlock, and the bullet ripped it off. Shouts of alarm were rising in the bunkhouse where

Aiken's home guard was turning in.

Hatfield kicked the door open and saw Len Purdue. The tall cowboy stood there with his hands shackled to the wall.

"Jim!" he growled. "I don't savvy. What is this, a trick?"

"Trick? Yuh'll soon find out if they make the door before we're clear!"

The chain was fastened to a staple driven deep into the wall. Hatfield had to shoot again to break a link, in order to free Len.

"Outside, quick!" he snapped, shoving the waddy before him. "There's a hoss waitin' for yuh at the northwest corner of the main pasture. Run for it, I'll cover yuh."

"Stop! Who the hell's that?"

The bellow came from an advance gunny who tore from the bunkhouse, a shotgun in his hands.

Chapter XIV
A Change of Heart

Moving figures emerged from the prison hut, and the gunny guessed it was an escape. Throwing up his gun, he let go. The scattering pellets peppered the Ranger and Purdue, stinging, some biting into the flesh.

The wounds, however, were not deep.

"Lucky that ain't buckshot!" Hatfield

muttered. For luckily the shotgun had been loaded for birds, or it would have been a more serious matter.

His Colt rose and boomed, and the shotgun artist had no chance to let go his second barrel. Three more men, pistols in hand, appeared, and started to shoot in his direction, but he had made the corner and got the thick-walled log hut between his hide and them. Their bullets only tore off splinters or sang past him in the air.

A couple of well placed slugs sent them reeling back for the shelter of the door, as more of their pards sought to rush out. In the brief confusion, Hatfield ran full speed along the wall of the hut, passed the smokehouse, and crossed the space to the pasture fence. Once he leaped this, they had to move well out from the bunkhouse before they could see him.

Their shouts and the explosions as they let go at vague objects, a pole or bush, anything that to their aroused imaginations might be a man, rang over the Ring A.

Purdue ran ahead of the Ranger, the light chain clanging. Hatfield overtook the waddy and pointed out the waiting mustang.

He ripped down a couple of bars, and Purdue, mounted, put the bronc at it and was outside the enclosure. A whistle from

Hatfield fetched the golden sorrel.

Their pursuers had located them now, though. Bullets were plugging the dirt, or whistling by them. One nicked Purdue's bare head, clipping his hair and burning his scalp. It dazed him for a moment, and the Ranger reached out, steadied him as they rode off.

"Jest a scratch, Jim," panted Len Purdue.

"Then ride! Ain't many of 'em, but no use takin' chances!"

They hit a trail and rode fast, and soon the Ranger realized they were not being followed. Most of the gunnies of the Ring A had ridden forth with Aiken and John Hawk. The few remaining dared not venture too far into the dark chaparral. The Ranger had killed one and wounded another, and those left behind were not the best fighters.

He pulled up, then, and set about getting the cuffs off Purdue's wrists. It took some minutes, and Len did not say anything as Hatfield worked.

"Why do yuh do this?" the waddy finally asked, as he arose and shook himself.

A shaft of light from the newly risen moon struck his swollen, bruised face. He had taken a lot of punishment from Aiken and Hawk.

"What yuh mean, why do I do it?"

Hatfield studied the young fellow's burning eyes. Then the explanation struck him, and he chuckled.

"Oh, I savvy! Yuh're ridin' under the same mistaken notion Dan Chock had! Yuh believe I'm one of Aiken's men!"

"Aren't yuh? Yuh killed General Drew Simmons. A man in Girvin seen yuh."

"Yeah? Who saw me?"

"Rabbit Withers, his name is. He claims he took a shot at yuh, while yuh was outside Simmons' winder!"

"So that's it! I didn't savvy it all."

It was, he had to confess, a clever plan. Withers was no doubt one of the Emperor's hirelings, a spy used by Hawk in Girvin. That was why they had discredited him, made it impossible for him to rally the decent men.

He explained to Purdue, who listened, unbelievingly at first. But when Hatfield brought out his Ranger star, and told the waddy the story, Purdue gave a cry of joy.

"You're Jim Hatfield! Why, shore! I've heard of yuh, Jim, of yore cleverness. 'Course yuh wouldn't've rescued me if yuh was in with Aiken! I been a fool ever to doubt yuh."

"C'mon, then. It's time we moved. I can lend yuh a spare gun I got in my bag."

"Where we goin'?"

"To stop a mass killin' that Hawk and Aiken plan. I ain't shore where it's to take place, but it's agin Tydin's and his bunch."

"So that's it! I heard a couple of 'em talkin' of a massacre!"

They mounted, and Purdue rode bareback, with a Colt stuck in his pants belt. Southward they hit the trail, parallel with the one on which the great army of gunnies had left the Ring A.

"I seen that young Gillette lady," remarked Hatfield, as they trotted forward. "She's right purty, Len."

Purdue stiffened, shook his head sadly.

"She is, Jim — but I'm 'fraid I ain't got much chance. Aiken was there first."

"Yuh may be right," drawled Hatfield. "She's hitchin' up with Aiken tomorrer."

Purdue cursed in dismay. "Marryin' him! Oh, damn the Hawk! Why didn't he kill me when he had me?"

"Easy," the Ranger told him. "I'm aimin' to be at that weddin'. Pull yoreself together. We got work to do."

He watched the cowboy fight back to self-control, and was satisfied with how he bore ill news, knew he could count on him.

As they rode on, the Ranger not daring to go too fast since he did not want to tread

131

on the Hawk's heels and betray his presence, he talked with Purdue in low tones.

"Tell me more about yore brother who got killed," he said.

Purdue told him how Frank Gillette had found the watch near the cave which the Ranger had already investigated. Hatfield kept what he had himself come upon locked in his mind.

The first light of the new day found them up on the ridge near the lake. Dismounting, Hatfield climbed a tall pine and scanned the country.

Rolling mists issued from the deep river canyon, leading from the reservoir. These hid the barranca for the time, but he could make out a bunch of mustangs, a couple of hundred of them, held up on the brink level not far from the dam. And he noted the furred black Stetsons of a dozen Aiken killers, keeping the animals quiet in the woods opposite his eyrie.

He descended and squatted by Len, who had spruced himself up as best he could.

"They're in position, Purdue. Yuh savvy Tydin's' battle plan?"

Len shook his head. "Not much of it, Jim. It was to be secret. The day of startin', the route we was to take in to the Ring A were close guarded, on account of spies. One thing I did know. It would have to be roundabout so's we could get in near enough to hit at night. The Hawk would spot us comin' if it was day."

"Yeah, it'd be tough, tryin' to slip a big bunch of riders through, close enough to hit that gang right. I'll have to wait till I see what goes on down there, and this is the best place, I reckon."

The two companions were hungry and began to chew on hardtack and strips of beef which Hatfield produced from his capacious saddle-bags. He always renewed his supplies when he could, for he was often caught out where he couldn't get a meal and could not use a rifle without warning nearby foes.

The warming sun would clear away these mists, and Hatfield again went up the tall pine. Now he could see into the canyon, and from his vantage point he caught a scintillating flash, the touch of light on metal.

"There they are!" he muttered.

Scores of murderous gunnies, hired by the Ring A, were up on ledges on trail side east of the ravine, spread along for hundreds of yards. Their rifles and shotguns were trained on the path which wound along below. At pointblank range, they would be able to riddle men riding that way — take most of them with their leaden hail before any warning came, and ruin the survivors in the jam and stampede that would ensue after the first withering blasts.

"No wonder they call it a massacre," he thought tightly.

He glanced down, and Purdue was staring up at him. He signalled and the waddy came up, stood on the brown limb below him.

"Yuh see 'em?" growled Hatfield.

It was nearly a mile to the killers, but the air was clear and both had the keen eyesight of frontiersmen.

"Shore, they're —"

"And here comes Tydin's' army!" exclaimed Hatfield.

Winding in a snakelike line through the gap, screened from the surrounding country on the level of the brink, appeared the men of Girvin, armed with rifles and pistols, heading in to do battle with the usurper of public lands, the man who had ruined Girvin, the Emperor of the Pecos.

"My Gawd!" gasped Purdue. "They'll slaughter 'em, Jim! We got to stop it! Fire yore gun, quick!"

"No," snapped Hatfield. He was already starting down. "We got a few minutes before they come to the narrow part. A couple of distant gunshots will only make 'em hurry this way!"

He realized the impossibility of warning the victims of Aiken's clever trap. It was too late to contact them before they rode in. He would have to break through the slow going dense chaparral, for if he crossed and took to the ravine, the killers would get him easily!

Chapter XV
Massacre Glen

Faced with a terrible decision, the Ranger had to make it swiftly. He must save the Girvin men, somehow, anyhow. Guns wouldn't do it, now. They would only push forward on hearing them, thinking the enemy coming.

"Werner and the colonel must've seen the advantage of movin' in that slit," he thought quickly, "and hoped to make it before they was spotted!"

But this was no time to think. He had to act! He went rapidly to work, snatched up the dynamite stricks, fuses and caps that he had picked up at the cave over at the Square G.

Purdue followed him, puzzled, as the Ranger sped down the slope, sliding, half falling, righting himself. Hatfield was oblivious to any danger to himself as he made this final play to snatch certain victory from the hands of Hawk and Aiken.

The high, but deep dam, which held in the waters of the lake, was built of huge boulders, with great pine logs for facing. There were plenty of wide cracks in the breast, and Hatfield, with an engineer's eye, quickly set his explosives as best he could in the short moments he had.

"Look out!" warned Purdue. "They see yuh — them hombres with the hosses!"

A bullet smacked into a log, a foot from the crouching Ranger. Len Purdue yanked his hogleg and began shooting at the men with the gang's horses, up on the ravine top.

"Be ready to run!" ordered Hatfield. "These fuses are short as hell!"

He began to light them, touching them off, and the sputtering lines hissed warningly.

Slugs sought the two men as they scrambled up from the dam breast and headed for the tall pines again. They could hear shots and shouts.

A mighty roar, and Hatfield was knocked flat on his face, stunned. A second came, and he was rolled over and over, unable to stop himself. He struck against Len Purdue who also had fallen and lay there, dazed.

The third stick of dynamite went off — and then rubble and bits of stone began raining on them.

"Keep — yore head down — and face covered," gasped Jim Hatfield.

Rocks threatened to finish them. The rattle of pebbles and dirt sounded on the leaves and grass.

The whole face of the dam was burst asunder by the explosives. It rose into the air, then the high wall of lake water, under great pressure at the constricted gap, rushed forward with a growing thunder.

The suddenly augmented river drove madly through the confining rock walls — a murderous tidal wave that swept great boulders and logs before it.

Hatfield got to his knees, wiping dirt from his eyes. He gave Purdue a hand, and the two men staggered up into the pines. The Ranger started to climb the tall tree, where he could see, and Len came after him.

In silence they watched the effect of the Ranger's desperate play.

The flood crest was upon the concealed Ring A outfit before they had any idea what the dynamite explosion meant. The gunnies were not far enough up the sides to escape the snatching skirts of the torrent. Many of them were swept off, carried on down, although the larger part of them managed to cling to projecting rocks and save their hides.

The forces from Girvin had, as Hatfield had predicted, started riding forward at faster speed when they heard the shots, though the explosions had puzzled them. They were still in a wider part of the gorge and, as the water breast appeared, many of them were able to ride up the sides. Others were picked up and carried on down, their mounts struggling to keep above the surface.

The widening of the ravine, on which Hatfield had counted to save the Girvin men, dropped the crest and diminished the force. Few of the men from the town suffered more than a wetting.

"Let's get down there," ordered Hatfield.

The stunned gunnies were picking themselves up. Arms and ammunition had been lost, and the projected massacre forgotten. The Girvin force, splitting up, could not continue longer in the canyon, but were trying to get out on the other side. For a time, as the flood slowly diminished, but the lake kept emptying and maintaining a high level over the trail in the bottom, the Ring A gunnies were stranded on their ledges.

Across from them, Hatfield and Purdue

began peppering them with pistol slugs.

"Yuh shore washed all idees of fight outa both sides, Jim, for the time bein'," Len Purdue said, chuckling.

Their Colts roared as they blasted at the foe across the deep canyon, still high with rushing muddy water. The lake was emptying through the gap, the level rapidly falling.

A few of the Emperor's gunnies who had held onto their weapons answered their fire, while the handful of men who had been watching the gang's mounts, grabbed lariats and hustled to assist their pardners in climbing out of the trap.

Large groups of mustangs were left practically unguarded, many of them but half-broken, and Hatfield was not the strategist to miss such a chance.

"Let's put a few slugs in over the heads of them cayuses, Len," he suggested.

Skillfully placed bullets started the horses rearing and dancing. Within minutes they were milling in the woods, and before the guards could get back up to stop it, a full-sized stampede began. Mustangs sped off in every direction, urged by the shrieking lead of Hatfield and Purdue.

"It'll slow any pursuit they try to organize," muttered the Ranger.

"Yuh shore saved the Girvin men from a nasty beatin'," complimented Purdue. "They'd've been slashed to ribbons in that barranca, Jim, if yuh hadn't thought of the water trick!"

Hatfield had no time to consider compliments. He was aware that the fight was only starting in earnest. The Emperor's army, though wet, could be rallied quickly.

"We got to work fast, Len," he said. "We'll pick up our hosses and ride down to the wide part below. They ought to be able to swim the river by the time we get there."

Already the flood was subsiding to some extent as the lake dropped.

Mounted, the two pushed through thick brush where long thorns ripped at leather and flesh. It was tough going, but finally they found a place of descent and got down to the edge of the muddy stream.

"C'mon," commanded the Ranger, putting Goldy to the torrent.

The rushing waters pushed against the mighty sorrel's body as he launched himself and swam for the other bank. After passing midstream, Hatfield glanced back, saw that Purdue, whose mustang was not so powerful as Goldy, needed help. His horse was floundering, being swept down. The Ranger quickly tossed his lariat end to Purdue. With this aid, both reached the opposite shore and climbed to the rim.

The bend and the heavy timber hid them from the gunnies above, and none of the Girvinites were in sight at this point.

"Pronto, now, Purdue," ordered Hatfield. "Ride down and fetch Tydin's and Werner to me here. I'll stick by these rocks so's to hold any of Hawk's gunnies who may try to get down on the citizens before they pull themselves together. Tell Tydin's and the mayor a Texas Ranger wants 'em, and to come fast. It's life or death."

Len nodded and kicked the mustang's ribs. He galloped along the chaparral-fringed, winding edge of the ravine.

Hatfield took from its secret pocket the silver star set on silver circle, emblem of the mighty Texas Rangers, and pinned it to his shirt.

Within a few minutes, as the Ranger kept a wary eye cocked upriver, rustling of brush from the other direction made him swing, and he saw Len Purdue hustling back, accompanied by Colonel Val Tydings on a big steel-blue stallion, and Mayor Abe Werner in his wake.

The two chiefs of the Girvinites stopped suddenly, staring at the cool, tall man who awaited them with the light glinting on his

Ranger badge.

"What!" shouted Tydings. "You! You a Ranger?"

Abe Werner's hand half rose toward the butt of his six-gun, and his deep-set eyes glowed angrily.

When they had taken the field against the Emperor of the Pecos, both Tydings and Werner had donned chaps and jackets to foil the tearing thorns of the Trans-Pecos. On Tydings' carrot-topped head was strapped a huge white Stetson. Guns rode at his blunt, stocky waist, and his feet were encased in muddy, square-toed boots, with long-rowelled spurs at the high heels.

Werner had on a sandy hat, and leather outer garments.

"No time to argue, Tydings," Hatfield said shortly. "Hawk and Aiken had two hundred gunnies on the ledges above the bend. They'd have wiped yuh out. I blowed that dam, as the only way to bust their ambush and save yore hides."

"Why, yuh —" gasped Abe Werner, searching for words in his anger.

"You fool!" snapped Tydings. "You have drowned us all! My men are all washed out —"

"No time to palaver," insisted Hatfield. "Hawk and Aiken were all set for yuh, guns loaded. If I'd shot warnin's, the firin' would jest have made yuh hurry on into the trap. Whip yore men together, Colonel, fast as yuh can and get 'em started downstream outa this. But don't cross the Pecos. Swing west and camp in them southwest hills, savvy? Yuh'll hear from me before long, and we'll hit the Ring A right!"

CHAPTER XVI
ONE-MAN STAND

Val Tydings' strategy, to move up on the Aiken forces through the deep canyon and thus get within striking distance of the huge spread, so that the Emperor's stronghold could be attacked at night by surprise, had failed. The enemy had learned the plan and set an ambush, only frustrated in their deadly work by Hatfield's quick thinking.

Tydings shrugged, as though this were too much for him. The men of Girvin had been convinced this big man had shot General Drew Simmons, and the brush with Dan Chock, coupled with the fact that Hatfield had been seen riding with Marshall Aiken, had cinched it.

"Rabbit Withers," the Ranger told them, "is a spy for Aiken. That yarn was cooked up to discredit me. Yuh must savvy yore town's full of Aiken agents."

"That's so," growled Abe Werner. "But why'd yuh ride with Aiken?"

"To learn his ways," snapped Hatfield. "But I tell yuh there's no time to lose. Pull yore men together, Tydin's! Run into them hills and wait for me."

"Where you goin'?" demanded Tydings. "We may need your help, Ranger."

Hatfield was already swinging the sorrel. He looked around. His wide mouth was grim, his eyes like icy chips.

"First, to delay Aiken and Hawk from catchin' yore men while they're disorganized. Yuh'll learn later what else. Purdue, stick with the colonel."

He waved his slim hand, and rode swiftly back up the river.

Hatfield checked his guns. The sun was warm, and he was drying off quickly. He figured that Tydings needed but a short time in which to pull his band together and get them out of danger, and he meant to give them that.

He knew the strength of Marshall Aiken, abetted by the savage cunning of John Hawk, the Emperor's chief of spies and leading killer. If they could manage it, they would seek to take advantage of the temporary disorganization of the Girvin fighters.

With a few experienced gunnies, a great deal of damage could be done at the right moment.

The sorrel raised his head, sniffed. The Ranger slipped from his saddle and got his carbine from its waterproof sling.

"Yeah, here they come," he muttered, as he glimpsed John Hawk, whose dark face was distorted in fury at the breaking up of the clever plot to massacre the Girvin men.

The breed was heading down from the point where half-drowned gunmen were being hoisted from the ravine.

There were a dozen men with Hawk, a handful quickly got together and mounted on mustangs easily caught. In close formation they were riding downstream, seeking to come up on top of the scattered Girvinites and do as much damage as possible before Tydings reformed his army.

Hatfield dropped behind a cluster of red rocks and whipped carbine slugs at the oncoming gunnies. A lean man whose form shielded the Hawk, crashed from his saddle with a shriek, while the Hawk's mount, clipped by a tearing bullet, went down on his knees, the breed sailing head-first into a thick mesquite clump.

The group broke, scattering, seeking shelter. A burst of return lead rattled about the Ranger's refuge. He stayed down for a moment, then bobbed up to send a plum into another of Hawk's killers.

The terrific gunfire of the Texas Ranger checked the small bunch of hard-riding devils. Shouts of hatred rang in the air, and lead whistled as they sought to destroy their arch-foe, Jim Hatfield.

They could not come on him from the ravine side, and the rocks prevented a frontal assault. He watched keenly, for he knew the cleverness of the Hawk. The breed and his men were, he found as he caught the crackle of dry brush, trying to circle and cut him off. He poured rapid bullets into the chaparral, heard a yelp, and a man fired at him from a sharp angle.

"Have to fade back," he muttered.

Down low, he scooted from tree to tree, and reached the golden sorrel. Leaping to leather, he spurred a couple of hundred yards down the river rim until he found another suitable spot to make a stand.

He nicked the Hawk's men, and slowed the bunch once more. Every minute counted, for it gave Tydings a chance to pull his men back out of reach.

More and more of the Ring A hireling fighters were riding in, piling up on the Ranger's deadly guns. He could hear John

Hawk's harsh, hate-dripping voice bawling orders to them.

"Get him! It's that dirty Ranger, boys! Fill him with lead!"

A bullet snapped at his Stetson brim, another bit a groove in his left forearm.

Slowly retreating, making them pay for every yard of the rough ground, Jim Hatfield delayed them until he figured he'd given Colonel Tydings and the Girvin forces plenty of time to withdraw. As he crouched back of his last rock nest, reloading his pistols, he knew that several of Hawk's hombres were trying to creep around him. They dared not ride into his sight, for his accurate shots cut down every gunny who showed.

Not far away, protected by a rise of ground and a thick clump of pines, waited the magnificent golden sorrel.

Jim Hatfield, stooped low, flitted back to Goldy and leaped to his leather. He drove straight away from the canyon, his revolvers blasting from both hands. For a few brief moments it was touch-and-go. He heard the Hawk hoarsely shouting to his followers, and one gunny sprang up, the round muzzle of his gun only a yard from the low-riding Ranger as he sped through. But Hatfield's weapon spoke a shade ahead of the outlaw's hogleg. The gunman teetered in his muddy boots, whirled and fell on his face.

Through the aisles of the bushy forest, guns roared hot and swift. But the line was thin, and then Hatfield was past, with only scratches paid in account.

He turned in his saddle to shoot back and shake them from any careful aim. He glimpsed the fierce, twisted face of the dark-skinned breed who thirsted for his blood.

His parting volley sent the Hawk ducking for shelter behind a thick tree trunk, as Ranger lead bit off the bark and sent dirt flying around the breed's boots.

Hatfield sped, hell-for-leather, in and out through the slim openings in the woods. They were all behind him now, and he was sure that the Girvin forces would reach safety.

Hatfield was plotting a course of action so that he would be sure to win the decisive battle against the forces of evil dominating the Trans-Pecos. By his swift, unerring work he had saved the Girvin men from annihilation, for had he not washed out Hawk's gunnies, the glen would now be filled with dying, slaughtered citizens, and the Emperor's power cinched.

He rode on toward the Pecos, keeping to thick ways as far as possible. Some springs spread out into a marsh with a sandy-bottomed stream emptying into it, and this covered tracks. He came out on shale at the base of a rusty-red escarpment, further hiding his sign from the keen eyes of John Hawk, in case the breed tried to trail him.

"Mustn't forget this'll be Aiken's weddin' night, Goldy," he told his pet. "Yuh reckon Hawk'll be best man?"

He worked up close to the valley in which stood the Square G, but turned north and got up on the heights where he had investigated the mysterious cavern before which Purdue had found his dead brother's watch. He could see the distant Gillette place now.

"They ain't here yet," he decided. "I s'pose Aiken and Hawk figgered on finishin' off the colonel's army first. Business before pleasure!"

His keen eyes sought the valley, noted a few buckboards and wagons slowly coming in. He could make out the skirts of women. Neighbors arriving for the wedding, probably.

"They shore had that massacre down pat," he muttered. "Hawk's spy system is well-nigh perfect. Aiken and the Guv'nor have got everything sewed up!"

Stock ran all over this section. Steers were up the draws and popping the bush at the slightest fright. He also observed horses, with Ring A or Square G brands on their hides and, taking his strong rawhide rope from its place in front of his right leg, he made ready for a cast.

Goldy knew this kind of work, and these mustangs were not wild ones, but domesticated and shod riding stock turned loose to forage. Thus the task of roping one was not difficult. Hatfield's loop soon settled over the head of a chestnut mare who quickly quieted down as he drew up and rode in on her, soothing her with his soft voice. He had a way with horses, and she accepted an improvised rawhide halter that he fixed from strips from his capacious bags.

Unsaddling, the Ranger turned his sorrel loose, but left the mare tied near at hand.

"Keep outa sight, Goldy, and don't stray far," he told his golden horse.

Wrapped in his blanket, with head on saddle, and gun close to his slim hand, he slept through the afternoon in a dense mesquite thicket.

Chapter XVII
Frontier Wedding

Not far above the western horizon, the sun was about gone when Jim Hatfield awoke. Creeping out on a high rock bluff, he peeked down into the valley where stood the Square G. Coming in from the west he noted a number of men, a dozen gunnies riding as bodyguard to Marshall Aiken, and behind them fifty more in the black Stetsons that was the badge of the Emperor's riders. The larger gang did not go to the ranchhouse but stayed a quarter of a mile out, guarding the entrance to the spread.

Hatfield made out the giant figure of Aiken, and the lean John Hawk, trotting his horse beside his boss.

"How touchin'," he thought. "It's the Emperor's weddin' night." The Ranger was hoping to kill two birds with one cast, the second bird a personal matter and perhaps small beside the chief one in importance. But he meant to do Len Purdue a favor — and Miss Peggy Gillette as well.

He had to wait till darkness fell, and it came suddenly as the sun dropped behind the far western mountains, plunging the velvet cloak of night over the wild Trans-Pecos. The air remained warm, sweet with aromatic plants, and as the stars twinkled into sight, cries of birds and other nocturnal creatures began. Far in the distance, a lone wolf howled mournfully from some barren peak.

A bite to eat, a drink of warmish water

from a canteen, and the Ranger was ready to start. Goldy came up at his low whistle, nuzzled his hand, and he saddled up but did not mount. The chestnut mare he had roped waited patiently, eyes sleepily closed, head down.

Hatfield took off his boots, changed to moccasins he always carried with him. Spurs and high heels were no good for the sort of work he had to do. He left his Stetson hung from Goldy's saddle-horn, and his leather chaps and jacket were also left behind. He must not be impeded.

With a lariat of tough rawhide, forty-five feet long, slung over his shoulder, the mighty Ranger started off and went on until he was well past the ranch. Locating a stout tree trunk on the brink of a cliff overhanging the valley he snubbed one end of the rope to it and let himself down behind the Square G.

He eased toward the brightly lighted house. To his ears came the lilting music of fiddlers playing at Marshall Aiken's wedding to Miss Peggy Gillette.

Women, neighbors of the Gillettes, had come from the far-spread reaches of the Emperor's domain. But men were in the majority, in this wild land. Whole barbecued steers had been made ready, cakes and bread had been baked by dozens in preparation for the feast.

Laughter and talk came to Hatfield as he stealthily advanced. There was a ring of light around the house, so that it would be difficult and dangerous to get in close. He wore two Colts, and his black hair was bound out of the way by his bandanna.

The kitchens were filled with volunteer cooks. The house overflowed up front with the guests.

Aware of the large band of gunnies a few hundred yards from the ranch, Hatfield moved cautiously. Hawk and a dozen picked hombres were in the house, and he must avoid them.

The daring scheme, which would have seemed mad had anyone else attempted it, had attracted the Ranger. He meant to match his skill against that of the Hawk and a small army of Aiken men.

One back corner of the rambling ranch-house afforded dense shadows, where a lean-to, used for tool storage, rested against the main structure. He watched his chance, and flitted in to it. Within a minute he had drawn himself up onto the low flat roof of the single-storied home, and tiptoed across, light on his feet as a panther. The noise below kept anyone from noticing any slight sounds his weight might make.

Hatfield suddenly froze, for he heard someone right beneath him, outside the house.

Close to the edge of the lean-to roof he waited, then realized that it was a woman below, and that she was sobbing her heart out. He flattened out and peeked over the edge. In the light from a nearby window, he saw Peggy Gillette.

She wore a wide-skirted, ruffled white dress, and a red wild rose was in her golden curls. Pretty as a picture, yet her small hands were over her face as she wept.

"Funny way to act on yore weddin' day," mused the Ranger. "Reckon I musta been right, at that!"

A heavy tread from the right, and then a gruff voice called thickly:

"Peggy, Peggy! Where are yuh?"

She turned, seeking to wipe away the tears as Marshall Aiken, in a new suit of fine blue cloth, and polished boots, came seeking her.

"Why, Peggy, yuh been cryin'!" he accused. "What's wrong?" The Emperor's heavy jaw dropped, and he scowled, his pride hurt. "What — yuh bawl like a kid 'cause yuh're marryin' the biggest man in these parts?"

Aiken had been drinking freely in celebration of his wedding, and was a bit unsteady.

"No, Marshall, no," Peggy cried. "It — it's just I don't like to leave Dad and — and Frank."

"Oh, I savvy." Aiken's face cleared, and he put his arm around her and kissed her lips. The girl tensed, but she did not try to stop him. "I was lookin' all over for yuh," went on Aiken. "Hawk said he'd seen yuh come this way."

"Peg-gy! Peg-gy!" a woman's voice sang out from up front. "Come here this instant!"

"Oh, that's Mrs. Mills calling me!" exclaimed the girl. "I forgot I promised to look at the cake."

She gave Aiken a fleeting smile, ducked under his arm, and ran lightly toward the front.

"Uh," grunted Aiken.

The Emperor took out some brown papers and a sack of tobacco, and began trying to roll a cigarette by the light from the window. He was close under the Ranger who, lying flat on the low roof, could have reached down and touched him. Aiken spilled a good deal of tobacco, and he swore.

The fiddle music, laughter and babble of voices rose high inside, and Hatfield took his chance.

Heavy Colt in hand, he struck down,

155

unerringly, the steel barrel connecting with a sharp crack against the Emperor's skull. The shock folded Aiken up, and he rolled against the house with a feeble grunt, inert as a pole-axed steer. The faint sounds were drowned in the merrymaking.

Swiftly the Ranger prepared to descend. But with his usual care he looked all ways before pushing over the edge of the roof. And up front, he glimpsed a moving shadow.

He drew back, waiting. John Hawk came sidling along the side of the house.

The lean breed was one of the worst criminals Jim Hatfield had ever encountered. The man's brain was sharp and quick, and he trusted a great deal to animal instinct with that savage blood in his veins. And next to Marshall Aiken and the unknown slimy Guv'nor the Hawk was the Ring A supporter the Ranger believed to be most dangerous. A gun was in Hawk's thin brown hand. His leather creaked slightly as he moved, with a serpent's deadly grace, black eyes sheening as they darted about. It was Hawk's skill and fighting strength, his many tricks, the outlaw army he ran, which supported Aiken, and it was Hawk who was proving a most annoying thorn in the Ranger's side as he hunted a way to smash the Emperor of the Pecos.

He could see the breed's face, dark and forbidding, the curve of the hawk nose, shadows of sideburns sweeping to the high cheekbones.

Colt ready, Hawk slipped up. The denser shadow of Aiken's unconscious bulk took his attention instantly. Hatfield heard the Hawk curse as he recognized his chief, and knelt by Aiken's side.

"Why, damnit," the breed said in a low voice, "yuh're drunk! The night yuh marry the purtiest woman in Texas!"

Aiken's thick curls hid the bruise where Hatfield's Colt had struck. Hawk tried to lift Aiken, then swore again and straightened up, turning back the way he had come, evidently to bring some of his men, for Aiken was a heavy man.

As he passed just under the Ranger, Hatfield hit him with the gun barrel, full in the temple. The Hawk whirled, reflex action sending him falling against the wall of the lean-to.

"Sorry it wasn't a bullet, Hawk," muttered the Ranger, as he dropped lightly to the ground.

He dared not stop for anything, if he was to carry out his plan to take Marshall Aiken. Up the valley, Hawk had a small army set, believing nobody could pass in or out without being spotted. And a dozen gunnies were circulating inside the house, keeping an eye on things.

Hatfield lifted the mighty Aiken, got his shoulder under the man's middle and straightened. Staggering beneath Aiken's great weight, he hustled at the best speed he could make through the darkness toward the rear of the buildings and down the narrowing valley to where his lariat hung.

He worked up the steepening slope, and reached the rope, fastening it under Aiken's armpits. Shinning up the taut lariat, feet braced against the rocks, he hit the top. Using the tree as a fulcrum, he hoisted his prisoner up. Snubbing the rope, he got hold of Aiken's clothing and rolled him over.

Sweat poured from him at his exertions as he stepped over and fetched up the chestnut mare, Goldy walking obediently after him.

The Ranger had snatched Marshall Aiken right out from under the nose of Hawk and the bodyguard. He would have enjoyed having it out with the Hawk, but had not chanced it, for it might have defeated his primary purpose, which was to get his hands on the Emperor.

He slung Aiken over the chestnut mare's back, and hogtied him. Strips of rawhide cord fastened wrists and ankles and were then pulled tight under the mare's belly. He stuffed Aiken's silk kerchief into the man's mouth and bound it firmly with shirt cloth tied at the back of the head.

"Try and wriggle outa that," he muttered.

Aware that as soon as the Hawk woke up, swift pursuit would begin, he hustled away, making the best of his start, leading the chestnut mare, with Aiken helpless as an inert bale across her back.

When he came to, John Hawk would organize the chase, and Hatfield, knowing the lean breed's brilliance, did not doubt that within a few hours the Hawk would work out every move he had made, how Aiken had been taken from the ravine.

He was playing a most dangerous game, alone, against the powerful forces of the Emperor of the Pecos.

CHAPTER XVIII
A NEW COMMANDER

Cool break of the new day found Jim Hatfield far to the south, heading for the mountains into which he had advised Colonel Tydings to lead his fighting men and await the Ranger.

Marshall Aiken had come to, hours before. The Ranger, ahead on Goldy, could hear the muffled sounds the Emperor made, but paid no attention to them. He was in a hurry.

Suddenly he cursed. The river that he had flooded, to flush out the Ring A killers, was still miles ahead. The chestnut mare could not keep up such a pace as the great sorrel, and the thick chaparral had slowed them.

Hatfield, Stetson strap bunching up his strong chin, swung to glance back. Aiken's eyes were wide as saucers, and he was mumbling in his gag. He knew who had him, and his cold, fishy orbs stared at the grim, tall Texas Ranger whose will nothing could defeat.

"Me'n yuh'll have a little talk soon as possible," remarked Hatfield. "Jest now, somebody's comin'. I on'y hope for yore sake it ain't some particular pard of yores!"

He was already moving aside in the chaparral, for his keen ears had caught the clink of a stone rolling under a horse's hoof.

It was too soon, he thought, for the Hawk to have worked down so far. Daylight would be needed to follow sign at any speed.

Still, anything was possible where such a man was concerned, so Hatfield drew his six-shooter and sat his saddle, watching the trail for the approaching horseman, as yet invisible.

The man was galloping full-tilt, oblivious to what might lie ahead of him, and he could not be watching sign at such a pace. Then through a bushy vista, the Ranger glimpsed Len Purdue, low over his horse's neck, spurring westward.

"Purdue!" he called, pushing out onto the trail.

The waddy's mustang, wearing a borrowed saddle, snorted and shied at the appearance of the two horses on the trail. Purdue yanked him to a sliding stop. Dust covered rider and mount, while streaks of sweaty lather made furrows down the animal's flanks. Purdue had been riding hard.

"Jim! Shore glad to see yuh . . . By hell, yuh've got Aiken!"

In stunned surprise, Purdue broke off, jaw dropping, as he recognized the helpless prisoner on the chestnut mare.

"Yeah," drawled the Ranger. "It was his weddin' night, Purdue, and I was there. He came along with me, 'stead of gittin' hitched to Miss Peggy Gillette."

Sudden hope sprang in Purdue's eyes.

"Then — they ain't married!"

"It don't look like it, does it? But what yuh doin' over here? Is somethin' wrong?"

"Yeah, Jim, there shore is. The nearness of that massacre panicked 'em, and 'stead of

161

hittin' for the hills like yuh ordered, they rode south to make a crossin'. The colonel figgered Aiken and the Hawk would have the regular fords covered, so they couldn't git over up above."

Hatfield muttered a curse. He had worked out a plan of action, but this put a crimp in it. Speed was essential, yet instead of having a fighting force on which he might count, close at hand, he found he was still alone.

"Where's Tydin's now?" he growled angrily.

"They went into camp for the night. The men was wore out, Jim. They're down to the south of here, hidden in a big barranca that opens out to the Pecos."

"Huh! I'll have to see Tydin's and Werner right away. C'mon."

He swung the sorrel back toward the big river, and rode at full-tilt, Purdue flogging the chestnut mare on with his quirt, to maintain the pace.

The sun was overhead when Hatfield, guided by Len Purdue, approached the camp of the Girvin forces. They were challenged, and at sight of the Ranger, scowls darkened the faces of the men, and guns were brought up. Not yet did they trust him, despite Purdue's story, and what had occurred at the river canyon, retailed by

162

Werner and Tydings.

On the big officer's vest shone the silver star on silver circle, emblem of the Rangers. It was the badge of his authority, respected throughout Texas. One Ranger was worth an army it was said — and Jim Hatfield was worth a troop of Rangers.

He jerked the magnificent sorrel to a sliding stop and raised a long arm.

"Gents," he said, his voice reaching to them all as they sprang up to face him, "yuh've been told I'm Hatfield of the Rangers. That killin' in Girvin was done by a spy of Aiken's, not by me. I had come to contact General Simmons, and give him aid."

Dan Chock sprang forward, his face reddening under his bristling beard.

"How do we savvy yuh're tellin' the truth? Yuh winged me, and yuh was seen ridin' with Aiken and Hawk! Yuh may be a spy —"

Hatfield eyed him coolly. He shrugged, and turned to Purdue, who was leading up the chestnut mare with the burden on her back. They had been so busy watching Hatfield that they had failed to notice what came behind.

"That," drawled Hatfield, "oughta settle all arguments, gents. In case yuh don't know

163

him, meet Marshall Aiken, Emperor of the Pecos."

Dan Chock stared, jaw dropping. The men crowded around, stunned as they recognized the chief of the enemy forces, handed over to them, helpless, by the Ranger.

"By Gawd," gasped Chock, "it's Aiken, shore enough!"

Words might have failed to convince them, but this play of Hatfield's downed every doubt. If he had worked for Aiken, he would never have placed his employer in their power.

"Hurrah!" shouted Chock. "Three cheers for the Ranger!" He seized Hatfield's hand, pumping it. "I been a damn fool, Ranger! I hope yuh'll forgive me and the whole passel of us. We was shore wrong about yuh." His eyes suddenly snapped. "Why, that Rabbit Withers musta been lyin' all the way through, boys! Wait'll I get my hands on his scrawny neck!"

"It's true I rode with Aiken," said Hatfield, "to look over the set-up. Where's Tydin's? We got no time to palaver."

"Abe Werner and him saddled up and rode on ahead," Chock answered.

"How long ago?"

"Oh, half an hour or so. We was gettin' ready to foller. Tydin's wanted to scout the crossin', and the mayor went with him."

"I savvy."

Hatfield wanted to contact Tydings, and use the leader as an aide. The Girvinites were Tydings' followers, and it was the Ranger's habit to win over local chiefs.

He signaled Len Purdue.

"Keep an eye on Aiken," he instructed. "Don't leave him for a minute. I'm goin' to fetch Werner and Tydin's, then we'll go to work."

Hatfield swung the golden sorrel and galloped at top pace for the Pecos.

Hard riding took him through the deep, bushed gap, and he could hear the rushing water of the dark river, its throaty voice echoing in the high, frowning walls. For centuries the Pecos had been stained with the blood of fighting men — Spaniards, Indians, then the ever encroaching whites who came to dominate the scene.

Suddenly he saw Colonel Val Tydings sitting on a stone, his blue-steel stallion at his side. Tydings had his head in his hands and was swaying unsteadily. A patch of blood was on his cheek and the Ranger noted a swelling discolored bump.

"Howdy, Colonel," he sang out. "What's wrong?"

Tydings started, looking past him, blinking.

"I was thrown off my horse," he replied shakily.

"Where's Mayor Werner?"

"He rode on, 'cross the river ahead of me. He's scouting the trail to Girvin."

"Sorry yuh couldn't see fit to foller out my orders, Colonel," Hatfield said severely. "I got a good plan for takin' Aiken's gang."

"That's a tough assignment, Ranger!"

"It can be done, but we got to move fast. I've captured Marshall Aiken. He's back at yore camp now."

Tydings sought the gray-green eyes.

"You mean it?" he demanded. "You've taken the Emperor?"

"Yeah, got him last night. That oughta settle any suspicions yuh got against me. Don't blame yuh for 'em, seein' as how clever-like they was planted. But now yuh must b'lieve me."

Tydings shook his head wearily. He seemed crushed, beaten.

"I believe you, Ranger. But we can't hit the Ring A now. We're outnumbered two to one. I counted on a surprise attack, getting within striking distance through the river canyon, then riding in after dark. That chance is gone, they're fully warned, know we're here. The thing to do is return to Girvin and try to find more fighters."

Hatfield shook his head. "The thing to do is to end this Emperor set-up pronto, Colonel. I don't like to go against yuh, and I can use yore help. But we're attackin'!"

A brick-red flush came up over the stocky man's face. He had a will of his own, was used to command. Having been elected to take Drew Simmons' place, as chief of the Girvinites, Tydings meant to carry out his own plans.

"I'm leader of those men, Ranger," he said firmly, "and I won't run them into a massacre. The near-massacre in that ravine was too close for comfort. We'll cross the Pecos now and make better preparations to strike. Abe Werner was right when he advised caution."

Time, precious time that meant victory or defeat, was rapidly being lost, and Jim Hatfield, whose will was conflicting with that of Val Tydings, was not the man to hesitate. The colonel's nerve had been shaken by the narrow shave in the gorge, and he was still stunned from his fall.

"Hate to do this, Colonel," drawled Hatfield, "but I got no more time to waste, savvy? Git up and unbuckle yore gun-belt."

Tydings stared at the tall officer on the

golden sorrel. He muttered a curse, but shrugged, as he found himself staring into a Colt muzzle in the slim, steady hand of the Texas Ranger.

"Very well, sir! But you'll find yourself in hot water for this. I'm in command of the Girvin forces and you're exceeding your authority."

"I'll answer later, Colonel."

Under the big man's hogleg, the colonel slowly rose, unbuckled his belts, let them drop at his feet.

"Step forward," ordered Hatfield. "Yuh had yore chance. Now I'm takin' over!"

Chapter XIX
Master Strategy

Red mounted angrily under Tydings' tan. He was furious at the Ranger's usurpation of his authority.

"They won't follow you without my order, Ranger," he said tightly. "You'll run them into a death-trap. You can't get near the Ring A without being spotted by Hawk's guards!"

"Lemme worry about that. I'll have to tie yuh, Colonel. But I'll fix it so yuh're freed as soon as possible."

In his difficult work as a State officer, Hatfield had before run into opposition from citizen leaders who objected to his masterful ways — sheriffs and neighborhood chiefs who thought they knew better than he how to deal with their peculiar troubles. It was part of a Ranger's task to overcome such doubts and, enlisting local aid, push through to the desired end.

Tydings dared not buck the might of Jim Hatfield. Anyhow, that Colt was too steady, the gray-green eyes too alert. He had seen the big fellow in action and knew his speed, so did not relish a personal set-to.

"Put yore hands behind yore back."

Swiftly Hatfield tied the stocky colonel's wrists, and then walked him up on the shale to a ledge out of sight of the trail in the bottom. It was obscured by bush growing from frail footing of earth which had sifted down into the cracks of the rock. Here he secured Tydings' ankles, then lightly gagged him.

He hid the sign so far as possible, and drove the colonel's horse into the Pecos. The animal swam to the other side and climbed up the steep road.

Turning the sorrel, Hatfield galloped back to the Girvin forces.

"What's the colonel say, Ranger?" asked Dan Chock.

"That yuh're to foller me," Hatfield said

smoothly. "Said my plan was great and for us to start, you obeyin' my orders. Tydin's'll be along as soon as possible. He's goin' to scout the Pecos rim for awhile — make shore all's clear. Now, Chock, I got a job for yuh. Yuh've plenty of nerve, and this'll take some of it."

"Call on me, Ranger," answered Dan Chock.

Chock, like the others, was backing the Ranger to the limit, since they believed that to be Tydings' orders.

"Change clothes with Aiken, Chock," Hatfield said. "Yuh're 'round his size. . . . Now, gents, see that yore men have their guns loaded and ready. I want eighty with me. The rest're goin' with Len Purdue on a dangerous run. Pick yore volunteers, Purdue."

Purdue was at his side. In a low, rapid voice, Hatfield amplified his orders to Len Purdue. As Len heard the startling news of Tydings' seizure, his jaws dropped, but he kept the news to himself.

The Girvin army had come under the Ranger's spell. His capture of Aiken, and the supposed authority invested in him by Colonel Tydings, made them fully loyal behind him.

Aiken's gag was removed and he was given

170

a drink of water. He began to curse Hatfield with a rage that was horrifying.

"Damn yore filthy hide, Ranger," gasped the Emperor. "I'll tear yuh to pieces when I get yuh, and I will. I will! I'll boil yuh in oil! Yuh rate Injun torture for this!"

His ankles were being untied, so that his suit might be removed and transferred to big Dan Chock as Hatfield had ordered. He tried to kick the Ranger, but was held down.

"When yuh're ready to talk, Aiken," the Ranger said coolly, "jest let me know."

"Go to hell! Yuh can't break me, Ranger. I — I'll have the law on yuh for this!"

"Why, yuh claim to be the law this side of the Pecos!" drawled the Ranger dryly. "Mebbe I can git yuh to change it in my favor, Aiken. The way yuh been actin', I figgered anything went over here!"

A chuckle went round the circle of Girvinites. The struggling, swearing Emperor was divested of his garments, and Dan Chock's were put on him. Hatfield heard the jingle of metal in the coat pocket, and appropriated the Emperor's bunch of keys before passing the clothes to Chock, who pulled them on. The blue suit, new for the wedding, was thorn-torn and muddy from the night trip.

Freshly bound, Marshall Aiken was

171

hoisted to the back of a strong horse, while Dan Chock, in the Emperor's duds, mounted the chestnut mare which had given Aiken his undignified ride from above the Square G.

Hatfield again drew Purdue aside, stressing his instructions so that the young waddy wouldn't make any fatal errors.

"Make sure Chock plays his part well, Len. That chestnut mare has a nail missin' from the shoe on her left forehoof and a nick as well. John Hawk can foller such a sign as easy as if we left written directions!"

"I got it all down, Jim," replied Purdue. "I won't fail yuh."

"Don't forgit Colonel Val Tydings. When yuh're through, yuh can ride and release him."

"Right."

Len Purdue took the lead of his band, including Dan Chock. He swung south, while Hatfield, on the great sorrel, started his hundred men for the Pecos ford. With the fighting men at Goldy's drumming heels, they swept to the river and started across.

"I wonder where the colonel went to?" a lieutenant said.

"Oh, he rode on up the bank, I reckon," Jim Hatfield said, and shrugged carelessly.

On the east bank, with all his army over, Hatfield headed full-tilt toward Girvin town, the dripping mounts of the Girvin hombres stringing out behind him. Two picked men guided the gray horse on which jounced the hog-tied Aiken.

He was hoping to deal the Ring A a crippling blow which would destroy their power forever, and he was matching his wits and skill against John Hawk, one of the smartest trackers with whom he had ever dealt.

In many respects Colonel Tydings was right. The slightest slip, and the citizens might run into a death-trap.

But peril was as the breath of life to Jim Hatfield, the greatest fighting man Texas had produced.

Swift, hard riding took the eighty men on their mission of vengeance, screened from the Pecos by the dense mesquite. At a ford below Girvin town that afternoon, the Ranger recrossed to the west side of the Pecos and, telling the squad lieutenants to keep them coming as fast as possible, he spurted out ahead to check any warning by Ring A spies.

He was hitting straight for the Emperor's stronghold, counting on his strategy to have drawn off the Hawk and the bulk of his killers.

Well in the van, as his gunfighters urged their mounts up to the high plateau, the Ranger let Goldy run at his best speed.

After a two-mile gallop, he spotted a man riding at a mad pace on the trail before him. He could make out the black-furred Stetson and, as he drew in closer, and the fellow swung to look behind, he recognized the dark face of a Mexican he had seen at the Ring A when he had posed as a gunny and joined the gang.

The Mexican's eyes rolled fearfully as he saw the tall rider rapidly overtaking him. Low over his chunky mustang, the Mex gouged his horse's flank, quirting him cruelly over the head to get the last ounce of speed from him.

Hatfield drew a Colt, got it ready for action. The gunman had pulled a pistol and sent one back. The Ranger heard it sing yards to the right. The jolting pace was too swift for accurate aim, so he held his own fire until he was within close range.

This spy had been watching the ford. Hatfield had figured there would be one or more there. He was trying to get to the spread to give warning of enemy approach.

But as the great sorrel inexorably brought the grim-lipped Ranger in, despair seized the Mexican. He jerked his reins, turning off into the chaparral, the mustang hitting the thorny bush with a loud pop.

Hatfield's Colt snapped once. The Mex, his brown-jacketed shoulders a full target to the accurate Ranger pistol, snapped his head back and fell off his horse.

Hatfield pulled up for a moment. The man was dead, shot through the heart.

Goldy started on once more, as Hatfield went on, clearing the way for his followers. He reloaded his Colt as he rode for the Ring A . . .

The half moon was just peeping over the tops of the black pines as the Ranger assembled his band a quarter of a mile from the gates of the Emperor's spread.

He had caught up with another trail guard and taken him prisoner. He was sure that Hawk and the bulk of the gunnies were still out on the false scent he had so skillfully arranged. He needed a few hours start on the Hawk, and believed he had it.

"All right, gents," the Ranger told the dusty, panting men, who sat their lathered and weary mustangs that had been driven to the limit in the attempt to reach the enemy stronghold in time. "We're hittin' 'em, now. Foller me, and cut down any hombre who tries to shoot."

"Yuh shore we ain't goin' to run onto two

hundred guns, Ranger?" inquired an older citizen. "If they're all home, we're in for a hell of a hot reception!"

"I'll stake my neck on it," Hatfield told him coolly. "C'mon now, and keep yore guns handy. I'll stay a hundred yards out front."

He slapped one of the black-furred Stetsons of the Ring A onto his head as he pushed the sorrel toward the closed gates of the ranch. He had taken one from a victim, for this purpose.

A man sprang up before him, a Winchester rifle glinting in the faint light. He saw the black hat, and lowered the rifle.

"Who's that?" he called.

"Hawk's comin'," Hatfield sang out.

That instant of delay proved fatal to the sentinel at the gate. The Ranger was on him before, cursing, he tried to use his rifle.

A Ranger Colt flashed blue-red in the night and the rifleman, his Winchester driving its long bullet into the dirt, fell close to the sorrel's drumming hoofs.

Hatfield yanked the rope which swung the wide gates open, and his men came piling in behind him.

"Hit hard, boys!" he sang out.

Colts in hand, the Ranger rode along the tree-bordered lane to the buildings, guiding

Goldy with his knees.

The banging of guns at the gates had waked the gunnies on guard at the Ring A before Hatfield swung up, rounding the dark ranchhouse and heading for the quarters of the killers. A shout sounded from inside as he approached, and a couple of fighters jumped out, strapping on holster belts.

A bullet whistled past the Ranger's ear. His own revolver smoked in his slim hand, and the leading gunny crashed back against his mate, shrieking as he took Ranger lead.

Chapter XX
The Draw-Off

Of the hired strong-arm Ring A men, only twenty-five were at the ranch. Caught asleep by the sudden arrival of Hatfield and his fighting citizen forces, they tried to slam the thick-slabbed bunkhouse door, but the body of the fellow shot by the Ranger blocked it.

"C'mon, boys!" bawled the Ranger, leaving his leather, both guns in hand as he lit running.

With the Colts blasting a path, clearing the doorway, he drove through, leaping the corpse of the killer he had downed, and crouching in the darkness to one side.

"What the hell!"

"It's that big jigger!" roared an Aiken lieutenant.

Heavy guns boomed in the long building, pandemonium reigning as they hunted the Ranger with bullets. Flares from exploding powder showed them to Jim Hatfield. A slug cut a groove in his left forearm, but did not stop him as he dived behind the end of a bunk, his Colts blaring, shattering the nerve of the tough devils bucking him.

It was nip and tuck for moments. Fighting alone in the bunkhouse, he heard the tearing of lead through the wooden walls, hitting the floor and ripping splinters from the bunk he had picked for cover.

"This way, Girvin men!" he roared.

They rushed bravely into the mêleé. As they poured through the doors, both front and back, the Ring A fire was rapidly diminishing. Several of the more faint-hearted gunnies threw down their weapons, crying their surrender, flinging themselves flat on the floor.

Acrid powdersmoke filled the flared nostrils of the mighty Ranger. His Colts were hot in his hands. He felt the wind of a bullet that kissed his cheek, one that came from directly opposite, where one gunny held out stubbornly.

Hatfield let go a snap-shot at the flash, aiming low, for the man was squatted as low as he was himself. The other Colt never spoke again.

Suddenly the guns ceased blasting in the bunkhouse. Smoke drifted up, and only the moan of a wounded man cut the sudden quiet.

"Let's have a light," commanded Hatfield.

He found a match and struck it. The flare showed the bunkhouse filled with Girvin men, hunting their foes and gunnies who hadn't taken fatal lead, with their hands elevated.

"All right, you Ring A gents. Line up against that wall. Take their weapons, boys, and tie 'em."

He touched his match to a couple of candles.

Scattered shots rang outside. As the Girvin men rapidly secured the captured gunnies, Jim Hatfield dashed out of the bunkhouse to check the rest of the spread.

But most of the opposition had been concentrated in the bunkhouse. The Mexican servants had not fought long, when they had found the circle of citizens drawing in.

The Ranger and his men had captured the enemy stronghold! Placing his men, so that no one could get through to warn the big fighting forces outside, Hatfield ordered the Mexes herded under armed guards into a big barn and set his trap.

"Fetch Aiken to the ranchhouse," he ordered Slim Orville, the bald-headed Girvinite who had fought like a demon. "And I wanta talk to a couple of them gunnies."

"Shore thing, Ranger."

Slim obeyed with alacrity, for his admiration for Hatfield's fighting ability had grown by leaps and bounds — as it had with all the fighting men who had ridden with Jim Hatfield, Texas Ranger.

In the big living room of the ranchhouse, Hatfield had a drink. There was food in plenty for his forces. They would need a rest, and a meal, in order to face the full shock of John Hawk's attack, which would certainly come.

A stout, sullen-faced gunny, with greasy black hair and a black-stubbled face was shoved in under the gun by Slim Orville, and stood up before the Ranger. Marshall Aiken, too, was fetched in, still tied and gagged, and put in a chair in a corner at Hatfield's command.

"Why, howdy, Utah," drawled Hatfield. He had known the man during his own short employment as a Ring A gunman.

"Sorta took yuh by surprise, I reckon."

Utah cursed him. "Yuh Ranger spy!" he snarled.

"Easy, Utah. There's some things I wanta know. If yuh tell 'em to me yuh might get off without stretchin' rope, as yuh deserve."

Slim Orville, "Pop" Lewis, and some of the other Girvin men, listened to Hatfield as he questioned the man.

"Hawk had fifty men at Gillette's for the weddin'," the Ranger said. "When Aiken got snatched, the Hawk started to hunt him, but he sent messengers back here to call out his full bunch — that right?"

"Yeah." Utah shrugged. "Left me in charge of the home guard."

Marshall Aiken, eyes rolling, could hear all that went on. His fishy eyes shot flashes of hatred at the masterful Ranger who had put a crimp in his mighty empire. Hatfield nodded toward him.

"Loosen him up a little, Pop," he said, "and give him a slug of his whisky. He'll need it."

As soon as Aiken's mouth was free, he began cursing Hatfield again, but he took the drink. Utah stared at his employer with wide-open eyes, licked his lips.

"Now, Utah, who's yore real chief?" Hatfield shot out suddenly. "The one they call

Guv'nor?"

He was watching Marshall Aiken instead of Utah, though, and saw Aiken blink, and his heavy jaw drop.

"That got to him," thought the Ranger.

"Huh?" asked Utah in a puzzled voice. "Why, Aiken's the boss, and the Hawk under him, of course."

"Then yuh don't know the Guv'nor?"

Utah shook his head. Knowing Utah to be no mental giant, who could successfully dissemble, Hatfield believed he really had no idea who the Guv'nor was.

"How about it, Aiken?" drawled Hatfield, moving across to stand over his star captive. "Ready to talk? Who backed yuh, and supplied the brains?"

"Go to hell!" snarled Aiken.

The Ranger shrugged, turned away. He would wait until Aiken was fully ready to surrender before going after him again.

"Keep a close eye on him, Slim," he instructed. "Gag him agin when I give the signal. Run Utah to the bunkhouse and fetch me another."

A Mex knifeman was shoved in next. Hatfield spoke to him in Spanish, but this hired killer could tell no more than had Utah.

None of the rank and file had the slightest idea of what he meant when he mentioned the Guv'nor. Marshall Aiken's eyes were filled with triumph as he crowed:

"Yuh'll get yores, Ranger! Six bullets in the belly, soon as my men come home. The Hawk'll skin yuh alive!"

Hatfield ignored him and went on giving orders. Guns were checked, guards posted. Aiken's was no idle boast. John Hawk and scores of hard fighters were still to be reckoned with. Inexorably Fate clicked off the seconds as the mass battle approached. It would be life or death.

Jim Hatfield rode over to the stone springhouse, where the mysterious Guv'nor had met Aiken and Hawk. He dismounted, crossed to the rail fence, and climbed over.

He hustled over to the tree where the Guv'nor had left his mount, and started a search for sign. He discovered a couple of hoof indentations which made him knit his brow. He was plainly startled.

" 'Tain't possible," he muttered, and looked more closely, for he could read sign as well as any John Hawk.

Then he picked up a tiny white bead, identical with the one he had found in Girvin.

"He's the Guv'nor," he muttered.

Lips grim, he examined the trunk of the big tree. At shoulder level of a horse, he picked off several short hairs, and peered at these.

"Everything dovetails perfect," he growled, teeth gritting. "Damn his hide!"

He knew who to go after now, but first must come the clean-up. He dared not leave Aiken's powerful army and the Hawk on the loose.

Miles south of the huge Ring A, Len Purdue rode the rear guard, where the danger lay, with his score of men out ahead. Up and down they rode through mesquite ridges and draws filled with prickly pears and other cactus growths.

Acting under the Ranger's careful instructions, Purdue saw to it that Dan Chock rode on the chestnut mustang, whose track left plenty of hoofprints for John Hawk, the Indian trailer, and that they were not covered by the prints of the other horses.

"Huh," he muttered, as he topped a high ridge and swept the panorama with his eyes. "I reckon that ain't from the wind!"

Far behind, he saw a trail of rising dust.

"Get ready, men!" he sang out, and others called the order up the strung-out line of horsemen. "Chock, it's up to you to play yore part now. Get across that mustang's back, and I'll tie yuh loose-like. Act like yuh

184

was helpless, savvy? Hawk's got mighty keen eyesight, and that's him a-comin' or I've ate loco weed!"

"All right, Len," Chock replied obediently.

He lay across the chestnut's back, hands hanging on one side, legs on the other, while Purdue secured his wrists and ankles with a strip of rawhide, although he did not draw the knots tight. Purdue also fastened a piece of light-colored hide over Chock's darker hair, to make the illusion that Chock was Marshall Aiken more certain, from a distance.

"Yeah, with him far enough off we'll fool him all right," announced Len. "Hawk'll think it's the Emperor for shore!"

"It's a smart trick," Chock agreed. "Hawk'll trail us to hell and back till he finds his mistake."

Hatfield's strategy was working out as he had planned it, with Purdue following it to the letter.

"We'll hold the ridge, boys," Purdue told them. "It's a good spot. The Hawk'll be in the advance guard, shore, and won't have enough men with him to take us. He'll send for reinforcements and then we can fade back."

The men were ready, guns and cartridge belts filled. They had eaten and drunk as they had moved south, leaving an open trail for John Hawk and his men to follow.

Purdue watched the lower ridge to the north, with the horses held back out of danger on the other side of the bushy, sharp-edged summit upon which they were crouched. There were big boulders scattered around making good cover, and he spread his fighters along the ridge top.

Purdue abruptly saw a horseman mounted on a rangy gray mustang, top the other ridge, a mile away. Behind the rider quickly appeared three more black-hatted figures and next a bunch of six, pushing up to the crest.

"That's the Hawk," he muttered, and threw up his rifle, taking steady aim.

The Winchester cracked, the whip-like explosion snapping off on the soft, aromatic breeze.

John Hawk, the lean, sinister breed, spied the puff, and Purdue watched the gray rear up as Hawk beat him with his quirt. The waddy's slug had kicked up shale around the mustang's forehoofs.

"Let 'er go, boys!" shouted Purdue. "Vern, give 'em a look at Chock, and that chestnut, but pull 'em back quick."

Dan Chock, slung over the back of the mare, was shown for a moment to Hawk

186

who was hot on Marshall Aiken's trail, and then the chestnut was jerked out of sight behind the summit.

"Now!" Purdue commanded, and his fighters let go with their rifles.

CHAPTER XXI
MAN TO MAN

Grimly John Hawk's men crowded up behind him. The Hawk had gone out on the trail of the Emperor and the Ranger with the gang he'd had with him at the Square G, sending messengers to fetch his full army. Pushing rapidly on the sign, once he had managed to pick it up over the lip of the valley in which the Gillette place stood, he had overtaken Purdue and the chestnut.

But Hawk had not expected such resistance as this. He had believed the Ranger to be riding alone with his captured prisoner. Now, for an instant, it looked as though hail were falling on the steep face of the ridge, around the Ring A gunnies. A horse went down, the rider rolling over and over on the slope. One of the bunched gunmen fell dead from his saddle, and a couple more felt the sting of lead.

Purdue, peeking out, saw Hawk's swift reaction as he roared commands to fire. Bullets reached to Purdue's position, and spat on the rocks, flinging lead and stone fragments over the men. One Girvin man took a glancing bullet through the leg, and his curse rang out as the roar of the guns died out in echoes.

"They're backin' up and dismountin'," Len called out, trying again for Hawk.

But the bony, dark-faced breed was moving fast, and so were his killers. They were ducking behind the other ridge crest, unsheathing their long-range rifles.

The battle opened fiercely as Hawk spread his followers along the summit, and rifles began pumping long bullets into the Girvinites' position. Purdue had chosen a good spot, and Hawk evidently was awaiting his reinforcements before attempting to storm the score or more of men on the rocky ridge across from him. Until then, he was satisfied with just holding them there.

"He'll wait till the bulk of his men come up, I reckon," thought Purdue. "And when they do, it'll be ten to one!"

The time wore on, and Len Purdue thought, with satisfaction, that every hour he delayed Hawk and the Ring A's main force meant more chance for Jim Hatfield. In this entrenched position, Purdue figured he could hold out for awhile. Of course, when it grew dark, then Hawk could creep up on them, but he and his men would be prepared.

The tension was like a taut bow-string all through the hot afternoon. And near nightfall, Purdue noted that new bunches of black-hatted riders were joining the enemy.

Purdue scuttled back from his vantage point as bullets smacked about him, tearing chunks from the ridge top. He found Chock behind the rocks on the chestnut mare.

"My belly's gettin' tired, lyin' this-away, Len," complained Chock.

"Yuh'll have to stand it a little while longer, Dan," Len Purdue said. "We'll move back soon as it's dark, though."

He lost no time, as night cast its velvet blanket over the Texas wilderness, in pulling his handful of fighters off the ridge, retreating rapidly through the chaparral flats to the south. The jungle of thorned brush was a protection to them, but Purdue knew they must keep moving and swing over so they could escape across the Pecos.

Narrow trails led them through the chaparral. There was a ford across the Pecos some miles below, and Purdue kept edging toward the canyon of the great river. If Hawk cut them off now he would slaughter them in his fury when he discovered how

189

he had been tricked.

Dan Chock, unable to stand any more belly riding, and figuring he was protected by the darkness, rode upright. The Girvin men pushed on under the stars. A little later a half moon came up, giving a bit more light.

Purdue stuck in the rear guard, and twice gunnies on swift mustangs pressed in on him. Weapons flashed in the dark, bullets zipped in the chaparral. Every instant was perilous. Purdue took a chunk of lead through the fleshy part of his thigh that stung like fury, and he could feel blood running down his leg into his boot.

The shock slowed him up for a minute or two. To his left, Dan Chock was riding the chestnut mare, and Purdue's eyes were suddenly blinded as a brilliant flare exploded close to the moving Chock.

"What the hell!" he gasped.

In the instant's illumination, he'd had a picture of the scene. John Hawk leaped in, eyes blazing, gun up. He caught the mare's reins and whipped her around. The flare, Len realized then, had been gunpowder the cunning Hawk had set off, to pin them. Guns roared, and the shouts of men who felt lead rang with the echoing Colts.

The Hawk had worked around on their

flanks and had pulled this trick to show them up!

Purdue saw that John Hawk was staring at Chock, who was trying to swing his gun. The telltale get-up which had given to Chock the illusion of being Marshall Aiken was exposed!

Then the light died as the Hawk's pistol blared, and Chock gave a squeak of agony.

"Back, boys!" roared Purdue. "Stick with me!"

They were diving for the thick chaparral pell-mell in a wild effort to get away from Hawk and his bunch. Confused yells, and exploding guns ripped the velvet night.

Pistol in one hand and guiding his horse with the other, Purdue fought like a demon. But more and more of Hawk's gunnies were piling in on them. The waddy's handful of men scattered, riding furiously for their lives through the brush.

For agonizing hours Purdue kept on however. Then pursuit stopped, and dawn was graying the sky. The young cowboy paused on a high spot, stared back. Northward, he saw rolling dust, and knew that Hawk had called his hombres off, and was heading back for the Ring A.

"He musta guessed the Ranger's idea," Purdue growled, wiping dust and blood from his eyes.

A bullet had cut his hair, and blood had flowed down his temple to his eye socket.

None of his friends were in sight; he could only hope that they had escaped, as he had. He swung and trotted his torn, weary mount back to the spot where Hawk had struck.

Dan Chock lay there with a slug through his head. He had died instantly when the Hawk had shot him as the burning powder had flared up. Purdue found another dead friend, and a dying horse. He ended the animal's agony with a merciful bullet.

Then he turned toward the Pecos ford.

"I hope to Gawd I at least give Hatfield enough time!" he muttered. "The Hawk is shore hotfootin' it for the Ring A now!"

He made the best time he could to the Pecos crossing. Once at the river, he dismounted, let the worn horse roll in the shallows, while he set about bathing himself and tying up his wounds as best he could.

The sun was coming up, casting yellow rays into the deep canyon. Purdue straightened up, refreshed by the sight of the water. Some vultures flapped down the canyon, and he stared at the ugly birds, shuddering at what their presence meant.

From where his horse now stood in the

river, knee deep, he could see the sandbar at the base of a protruding red cliff, and then something caught his alert vision.

"Why, it's a body!" he muttered. "Now who's that?"

He dismounted and started wading down toward the still, inert body, washed up on the bar by the swerving current as it was deflected by the rock wall of the ravine. A man in leather lay on his face, arms out-stretched, head half buried in sand, legs in the water. In one hand he held what looked like a hide moccasin. And a yard from him was a big white Stetson.

"Colonel Tydin's!" gasped Purdue, recognizing the headgear.

Jim Hatfield came alert from the forty winks he had been snatching, as he waited guns ready in their holsters, for the return of John Hawk and his full force of fighting men.

Everything was set. The daylight hours had sped on, with the Ring A outwardly at peace in the brilliant Texas sun. Pigs, chickens and dogs basked in the warmth of the yards. In the corrals, colts frisked, while in the distance could be heard the bawling of steers.

With less than half the number of men the Hawk could muster, Hatfield was prepared. None of his army was visible outside. In the ranchhouse living room Slim Orville sat with gun in hand, watching Marshall Aiken. The Emperor of the Pecos lay on a couch in the huge main room, tied and a captive.

The thud of hoofs brought the Ranger up, and he touched the Colts in their supple, oiled holsters.

"Get that gag on Aiken pronto, Slim," he commanded. "Then skip outa sight. Signal the boys the time's come."

He took a stand to the left of the front door, and from a window could see the open gate down the tree-shaded lane. In a few minutes he sighted the bony, dark-faced Hawk spurring a bleeding, beaten mustang up the trail to the ranch.

"He's shore rode that bronc to a frazzle," Hatfield thought, frowning angrily. Abusing a horse always riled the Ranger.

John Hawk's dark, deep-set eyes darted from spot to spot, hunting trouble, but Hatfield had fixed it so that all looked peaceful and right at the Ring A. Evidently Hawk was satisfied, for he came straight on to the ranch.

A hundred yards behind appeared a dozen gunnies, while strung out still farther back more and more galloped worn-out mustangs for home, the trail jamming with them. All showed the effects of their long, breakneck ride to reach the Ring A.

Fooled by the quiet of the spread, the Hawk came to a sliding stop and left his saddle in a bound, running up the porch steps.

Hatfield stood close to the front wall on the side opposite to Marshall Aiken. He figured the Hawk would catch sight of his chief first of all, there on the couch.

The breed's dark-skinned face, with its high cheekbones and the curved nose, crisp mustache and straight, grim lips, appeared at the door. He jumped through it.

"Aiken!" he howled, as he saw the trussed Emperor. "How in hell —"

"Will yuh reach, Hawk?" Hatfield's voice snapped, concise and startling. "Or —"

John Hawk's breath came in a snarling curse as he glanced round and saw his tall arch-foe — the Texas Ranger, whose skill and strength had balked the grandiose scheme to hold the vast Trans-Pecos.

The breed's long-fingered, blue-knuckled hands hung loose at his hips. He carried two heavy revolvers, and a long knife. The muscles of his lean jaws tightened. His crisp mustache twitched as his black eyes fixed the gray-green eyes of Jim Hatfield.

195

It was only the fraction of a breath that these super-opponents stood immobile. They were separated by only a dozen feet as their powerful wills, one for good, the other for evil, clashed.

The van of the gunnies who had ridden with the Hawk were bunching up along the lane. The Hawk did not see anyone else — except Hatfield — and he made his play, win or die.

"Curse yore hide, Ranger!" he snarled.

The bony, blue-knuckled hand moved too fast for eye to follow, though Hatfield caught the twitch of an arm muscle.

Hawk's shining revolver flashed from its holster, hammer spur back under thumb. Its thunder roared through the room.

CHAPTER XXII
RING A BATTLE

Poised with his booted feet wide in a gun-fighter's crouch, Jim Hatfield matched his draw against the Hawk's. The Ranger Colt came to firing level that vital trifle of time that meant the difference between life and death. His slug smashed into the breed's murderous brain.

He felt the nick of Hawk's lead as it struck between his wide-set boots, grooving the leather of a sole. But John Hawk had failed to raise his long barrel because his brain which directed his movements had been shattered by Hatfield's bullet.

Hawk's black-furred Stetson, with the Ring A device in front, fell from his long-haired, dark head. The black eyes widened, by reflex action, glazing as he stood like a statue for a breath. Between the eyes was a round bullet hole.

Silently the breed folded up like a broken jumping-jack, his pistol rattling on the floor.

Hatfield let out a Ranger war-whoop and sprang across the dead John Hawk, chief of gunnies.

The fighting men of the Emperor were coming on now. The shots from inside had electrified them, and rough hands dropped to revolvers or reached for rifles in slings.

"The jig's up!" roared Hatfield. "Throw down yore guns!"

In reply, a gunny let go a hasty one that missed the Ranger by a yard and kicked a splinter from the house wall. Hatfield, both Colts out, replied, knocking the man from his lathered, bloody-flanked horse.

Then the gunmen were falling back, piling up on themselves, startled at sight of the tall man they had come to dread.

"Get him, boys!" shrieked a gunny lieutenant. "Fire!"

Hatfield scrambled back to the shelter of the house. He jumped through the door in the nick of time as a hundred bullets drove into the wooden walls and porch. The terrific roar of the guns rattled over the Ring A, which a moment before was quiet as death.

The volley echoed, and shouts of leaders punctuated the din as they gave their orders.

"Ring the house!" bellowed a black-bearded devil, both Colts smashing bullets blindly at the open doorway.

Jim Hatfield was leaping for the rear. Slim Orville, with a dozen picked fighting men dashed in, rifles up and loaded, to take the various windows.

Behind the house Goldy waited, saddled and ready to go, and the Ranger hit leather without touching iron. Gunmen were appearing from two sides of the house as they deployed to circle the huge *hacienda.* Hatfield's bullets stung them, knocked a man off his mustang from one direction, wounded the leader on the other wing.

Two lines of Ring A devils were coming along the sides of the great ranchhouse now. From the windows Orville's fighters opened up an accurate, deadly rifle fire that cut them to ribbons.

More and more gangs of gunnies were shoving up, putting pressure on those ahead, falling back as they realized their flanks were wide open.

With his Colts roaring defiance, Hatfield spurted Goldy to the shelter of a barn, rounding it to cut off a fresh line which had winged out that way. And as gunmen poured in to the yard from the bunkhouse, the store and other structures, filling the space, a concerted volley of Winchesters rattled.

Then the Girvin fighters set at strategic points, were in action.

Appalled as one after another of their number took crippling lead, as the shrieks of wounded men and horses rose in the hot air now clogged with billowing clouds of whitish dust, the Ring A halted.

The mêleé was frightful as the great mass of Ring A killers hurled themselves into a fiercely renewed battle — this time to extricate themselvs from the Ranger trap.

Swiftly reloading his Colts Hatfield spurred out, the golden sorrel a flash of yellow, mane and tail flying, the Ranger low over his back. Hatfield's aim was to single out the lieutenant sub-chiefs. He had marked them during his stay at the ranch.

Bullets sang about his ears, perforated his Stetson. A slug grooved the golden gelding's hide, and Goldy gave a terrific leap, faltered, then ran on.

From the buildings once more roared that terrible, soul-smashing volley of rifle fire, slashing the bunched gunnies. More than fifty had felt the lead of revenge for their murderous deeds. Another gang, to the rear, managed to get turned and, their bellies full of such fight and unable to do more than glimpse the Girvin men who riddled them, were starting to retreat to the gates.

The speed of the sorrel took Hatfield far ahead of the retreating gunnies. The gelding did not pause but flew over the fence, landing on the trail outside.

"Ready, gents!" shouted Hatfield to the hidden men waiting outside the gate. "Here they come!"

He streaked up the trail, grabbed the gate rope, and swung it shut as he passed, blocking hasty exit from the yard.

Bellows of hate and pain, screams of mustangs which had taken lead, the banging of hundreds of guns made the Ring A a bedlam in hell.

The van of the retreat hit the fence. Some went over, but others tried to open the gates. As they stopped, men sprang up in the chaparral fifty yards across the trail, rifles blaring.

Back at the house, rifles of the Girvin men steadily cut down the outlaws and killers who had been enlisted by Marshall Aiken and the Hawk to do their evil bidding.

Backing up as they found themselves faced by more Winchesters, the gunnies at the gate split in every direction, thinking only of escape. More were coming. They saw what was happening and pulled their mounts to a sliding stop, desperately looking about for another way out.

Hatfield, riding a circle, kept the gunmen bunched. He wanted to break them utterly, prevent any rally.

Colts blasting he poured .45 bullets into the mob, oblivious to the wild slugs that sought to pick him off.

At the ranchhouse, caught by the ambuscaded Girvinites, other gunnies were throwing down their weapons, and raising hands in surrender. The armed men in the house rushed out to make this section of the Ring A forces prisoners.

Some of the citizen fighters grabbed saddled horses and rode out in a spaced line to cut off any possible retreat. The shooting was dying down. Only scattered explosions sounded as some desperate killer, aware that hemp awaited him if captured, tried to break through the closing ring.

Jim Hatfield rode back into the big enclosure.

"Throw down yore guns, Ring A!" he roared.

Colts up and watching for any individuals who might at the last moment choose death rather than be taken, he led his horsemen into a wide circle that came in upon the shattered gunnies.

Pistols, rifles, and long knives were being cast to earth. The Emperor's big army was done.

As the firing ceased, clouds of dust and acrid burnt powder-smoke rolled slowly away on the Texas breeze. The sun shone blandly, warmly, upon the battlefield.

Hatfield's forces, sheltered during the worst of the scrap, had hardly been scratched. A few had bullets in their hides, and a couple had been struck fatally. But more than half the gunnies had taken lead.

Rapidly the Ranger herded his prisoners, under armed guard, while men started to tend the wounded. Then, grim-faced, Hatfield dismounted and entered the living room.

Marshall Aiken lay where he had been, his eyes wide with excitement.

Hatfield stepped over, snatched off the gag and untied his bonds.

"On yore hind legs, Aiken," he growled, "and go take a look at what yuh've caused."

"Damn yuh!" he shrieked. "I hoped — I hoped —"

Hatfield shoved him roughly ahead of him, a Colt in his hand — a Colt whose deadliness had shaken Aiken to the core. The Emperor had been brutal and efficient at murder, but now that he had finally been struck, he broke. His eyes rolled with terror as they kept returning to the still, bony form of John Hawk, whom he had believed the deadliest fighting man alive.

The Ranger threw the giant out to the porch.

"Take a good look, Aiken!" he snapped. "This is yore doin'."

With dropped jaw the Emperor of the Pecos stared at the battlefield, at the writhing wounded, the screeching, injured animals. He saw the havoc wrought among his men, and the balloon of his grandiose scheme collapsed.

"Stop, Ranger!" he begged. "I can't stand no more."

But Hatfield, a master at seizing opportunity, wouldn't let him rest.

"Talk, then, Aiken. Or would yuh rather I

did it for yuh? I savvy why the Hawk and you drygulched Gillette's son Phil and Purdue's brother. I can name yore 'Guv'nor' for yuh, the hombre who thought up this scheme and is really chief in the game yuh've played!"

Hatfield snapped a name at the shaking Emperor of the Pecos.

Aiken's fishy-blue eyes were round as agate marbles. He gulped, as he stared into the stern face of the man who had broken him, driven him into the ground.

"All right, I'll talk!" he choked.

It was night when Jim Hatfield, at the head of his fighting men, swung into the valley gap leading to the Square G. With them was the broken gunny army with hands tied to its saddle-horns and guarded.

Ahead he could see lights. With long lines of horsemen at the golden sorrel's proud heels, he headed his assistants to the lighted ranchhouse.

He had business with Gillette which he wished to conclude before crossing the Pecos.

"Jim!"

Len Purdue, sitting on the front step with Peggy Gillette, sprang to his feet, singing out in joy as he recognized the tall Ranger.

"Howdy, Len. Say, did yuh cut Tydin's loose?"

"I found his Stetson on a sandbar, below the south ford. Jim, I got somethin' to show yuh. Come with me."

He led Hatfield off from the house.

"I didn't want to stir Peggy up, Jim," he explained. "She's already had plenty worry. I got here awhile ago, and as there wasn't no Ring A gunnies here — the Hawk had took 'em all off with him — I come in. But I want yuh to see this."

A lantern burned low in a shed, and Hatfield trailed his waddy friend inside. Purdue stooped, pulled back a blanket from a body lying there.

"Huh," grunted the Ranger. "Been stabbed and thrown into the Pecos!"

"The white hat there was lyin' right by him," Purdue said. "The colonel must've rubbed his wrist bonds on a rock, I reckon, and got loose. I found this gripped tight in this here dead man's hand."

Purdue picked up a soaked moccasin.

"Good!" Hatfield nodded. "I been on the trail of this. I got it all worked out, Len, but I'm glad to get the moccasin. Look, see the busted thread? There's still a few of them small white beads stickin' on. The Guv'nor dropped 'em. I found a couple, and that cinched it for me."

"What yuh mean?" asked Purdue.

"I got to palaver with Gillette now," Hatfield said hurriedly. "Purty soon it'll all be made clear."

Hatfield strode from the shack, with Len at his heels.

"I'm mighty happy yuh're all right, Jim," Purdue said as they hurried for the front of the ranchhouse. "I was afraid mebbe I hadn't held Hawk long enough."

"Yuh done a fine job, Chock and you. The Hawk come to the Ring A, and we took 'em all."

"The Hawk, too?"

"He wouldn't give up," the Ranger shrugged. "Now he's done."

"Chock got killed," Purdue said sadly. Briefly he told the Ranger of the night mêleé.

At the steps they smiled at Peggy, and David Gillette limped to the open door.

"Howdy," he called. "C'mon in."

The Ranger went in, and at his order Slim Orville brought in the fettered Marshall Aiken. The fallen Emperor's face was sickly under his bronzed skin.

"I got a word to say to yuh, Gillette," drawled the Ranger. "Here's one of the murderers of yore son. Aiken and Hawk drygulched Phil and Harry Purdue. Yore son and Purdue's brother had located a gold vein in a cave on the north plateau — a rich one. I had a look at it and it's worth plenty. They kept it to themselves, fearin' Aiken would try to take it. Hawk smelt 'em out, and him and Aiken shot 'em. Then they killed a bunch of yore riders that had seen 'em — all but two spies they had worked in with yuh."

"So that's why Aiken wanted that land!" shouted Gillette. "I finally told him I'd give it to him for a weddin' present!"

"Yeah. Aiken wanted to win yuh over. Yuh've got a lot of influence on this side of the river, and were known to be friendly to him. Once hitched to yore daughter, Aiken could get yore gold. He needed it bad, to keep payin' his gunnies. That kind don't work for love, and he had a big payroll to meet ev'ry month."

The old man's eyes were darting daggers of fire at the cringing Emperor.

"Ranger," he said, "I been crippled, couldn't fight much, but I did figger I was watchin' out for my children. I thought Peggy loved Aiken, since she was marryin' him."

"Oh, Dad!" Peggy ran to her father, flung her arms about him. "I never loved Marshall, never! But I knew he was threatening you, and — I was afraid of Hawk! Yes, and of Marshall, too. I thought if I married Marshall it would save you trouble!"

She began to sob, her head on her father's big chest.

"The Emperor's broke now, and the Hawk won't kick up any more fuss," declared the Ranger. "I —"

Loud voices sounded outside, and Hatfield paused.

"Hey, Ranger!" sang out one of his aides. "Here comes a flock of riders!"

Chapter XXIII
The Guv'nor

Yells and confused calls rang in the valley. A couple of dozen riders, among them a sprinkling of the twenty who had been with Len Purdue when he had drawn off John Hawk, pushed toward the house.

Colonel Val Tydings, on his blue-steel stallion, was at their head. He dismounted and stalked inside. Under his wide brown Stetson his eyes were hard as they fixed the Ranger.

"You're under arrest, Hatfield!" he shouted. "I've wired your superiors in Austin of your high-handed doings."

"Take it easy, Tydin's," Hatfield said coldly, facing the furious man steadily.

"Damn you —" began Tydings in red-hot rage, but stopped short, eyes widening, jaw dropping as he caught sight of Marshall Aiken, a prisoner.

"Pin yore feathers down, Colonel," cautioned Slim Orville. "What's got yuh so riled?"

Men were crowding up, listening. Tydings licked his lips, braced his blunt figure as he leveled a finger at the Ranger.

"I was attacked by this man, I tell you. He stuck a gun on me, tied me up, and hid me in the rocks by the ford, but I finally managed to rub a rope loose. He meant to lead you into slaughter!"

"He done that, all right," interposed Orville dryly. "Only it wasn't us that got slaughtered, 'twas the Ring A. The Ranger's done smashed Hawk and Aiken, and we got most of their gunnies, too."

Hatfield signaled Len Purdue.

"Step out and fetch in the colonel's saddlebags," he ordered.

Purdue hustled out, and Tydings, furious as he found he was cornered, snarled: "That man's a killer! Hatfield shot General Drew Simmons!"

Hatfield, close on him, suddenly struck.

His fist connected with the prognathous jaw with a crack as sharp as a pistol shot. Tydings staggered against the wall.

"Yuh're cooked, Tydin's!" the Ranger snapped. "Aiken's talked — but I got on yore trail anyways! Yuh made a bad error, ridin' here into my hands."

Purdue shoved through the crowd, the saddle-bags in his hand. He passed them to the Ranger, who opened them, picking out spare bullets and various other belongings carried by Western riders.

"No moccasins now," he drawled. "Guess yuh throwed the mate away!"

He felt in the bottom of the bags, and brought out several small white beads. Then he drew from his hip pocket the moccasin which had been clutched in the hand of the drowned man on the Pecos sand-bar.

"Yuh can't deny this is yores," he accused. "It fits yuh, and yuh see the beads match. This moccasin was found in Mayor Abe Werner's hand, after yuh knifed him and throwed his body in the Pecos, jest before I come up on yuh. Yuh'd had a fight with him. He was suspicious of yuh — reckon he found a moccasin track near his house the night yuh tried to dry-gulch him! I s'pose he got real hot on yore trail, after that massacre. I understand yuh pretended yore stallion had picked up a stone, so yuh was well to the rear and wouldn't have got hurt in the massacre. That white Stetson yuh lost strugglin' with Werner would mark yuh for Aiken's gunnies, too, so's they wouldn't shoot at yuh — likely had their orders from Aiken."

Tydings stood frozen, eyes on the grim Ranger. Rapidly Hatfield drove home his accusations.

"Yuh Shot General Simmons so's yuh could control his army, lead 'em into the canyon trap. Dropped Werner's coat button to discredit him and make shore yuh'd be chosen chief. Tried to kill me and Purdue, sneakin' up in yore beaded moccasins. A thread on 'em busted. I found two beads that match these others perfect. I picked off several blue-steel hairs, from where yore pet fine stallion rubbed that tree by the Ring A the night yuh informed Aiken I was a Ranger! And the tracks all fit, Tydin's."

Spellbound they listened as the big Ranger totally damned Colonel Val Tydings.

"Yuh figgered out this scheme of makin' Marshall Aiken Emperor of the Pecos. Hoped to win an empire. Yore real name's Val Aiken! Convicted of a shootin' in Kansas twenty-five years back, sent to prison for life, yuh done eighteen years before yuh escaped. After floatin' around, yuh returned to these parts under a new name. Yuh'd changed a lot, and there were few folks left who'd ever seen yuh when yuh was young. Yuh'd deserted a wife near here, and she was dead, but yuh contacted yore son, Marshall Aiken, and set yore big scheme to workin'." His eyes bored hard into those of the colonel's. "These are facts, Tydin's — or Aiken — because they come straight from that son of yours!

"Yuh financed him with stolen money, and in order to make shore no opposition smashed the Ring A, yuh joined the movement agin it, all the time sendin' Aiken information and instructions. Finally yuh shot Simmons, and led the men into that murder trap. Rabbit Withers was one of yore town spies. He'll tell the truth 'bout Simmons' killin' when he sees yuh're a pris'ner and can't get at him. So —"

"Look out, Jim!" roared Len Purdue, leaping forward.

Peggy Gillette screamed, and ran across the room as she saw Purdue jumping between Tydings and the Ranger.

Val Aiken, alias "Colonel Tydings," suddenly bounded for the open door.

The stocky man, clever killer and thief, one of the slimiest criminals the Ranger had ever come up against, had flashed a Colt from inside his shirt. That snub-nosed weapon came as a surprise even to Jim Hatfield, who was expecting him to make a play for his guns that were in sight.

The Ranger had to snap one that wouldn't hurt any of the stunned, gaping Girvinites who had been listening in amazement to the officer's indictment of a man they had looked upon as a loyal chief.

His lips drawn back from his teeth in a snarl, a look that was familiar flashed across the stocky man's face. It was like the look on Marshall Aiken's face when he was cornered. Father and son.

"Stand aside!" bellowed Hatfield.

His Colt had come to his slim hand with its usual blinding speed, hammer spur back under his thumb. But he couldn't shoot for an instant because his arch-enemy had made good use of innocent men as cover.

A slug from the snub-nosed revolver tore through Len Purdue's shoulder. The young waddy faltered and fell on his face, blood oozing from his sleeve.

The second shot, with the way clear to Hatfield, bit a chunk from the shifting Ranger's ribs, but it did not stop him. His big .45 boomed, and Val Aiken, alias Tydings, doubled up in the middle, staggered against the surprised citizens, and fell among them. Willing hands swiftly seized the killer's guns.

"He's dead as a doornail, Ranger," growled Slim Orville. "Yuh got him in the heart!"

The tall, grim-faced Texas Ranger swung, pouching his Colt.

Before him he saw Peggy Gillette, kneeling by Len Purdue, holding the cowboy's head in her lap, kissing him.

"Oh, Len, I love you!" she was sobbing. "I've loved you all the time, from the first! Don't die — please don't die! I told Marshall I'd marry him right away, to save your life! He and Hawk would have killed you otherwise!"

A look of wonder came into Purdue's eyes. He forgot pain and everything else. In the whole world, there were just the two of them.

"Peggy! I — I ain't hurt bad, don't worry! I shore love yuh!"

Captain Bill McDowell waved a yellow telegraph sheet under the eyes of Jim Hatfield, back at Austin headquarters to report.

"Who is this here Colonel Val Tydings who sees fit to 'cuse my best Ranger of murder, kidnapin' and all the crimes in the pack?"

"Yuh'd be right, Cap'n Bill," drawled Hatfield, "if yuh asked, who was he? For he's pushin' up the bunch grass west of the Pecos now."

Leaving out trimmings, Jim Hatfield told McDowell of the hard fight he had put up against the Emperor of the Pecos.

"Marshall Aiken's goin' to prison, the rest are dead or gettin' the same dose."

"Then I reckon Texas kin still claim west of the Pecos as her own! Fine work, Jim!"

The old fellow's eyes beamed upon his star man who carried the law to the farthest reaches of the mighty Lone Star State. Then his face grew serious. He reached for a letter on his desk.

"I don't have to ask if yuh're all right, Jim," he said. "I can see it. Now listen to this — from the Border! And all my troops are out!"

Hatfield grinned, as he rolled himself a smoke. He could read his Chief like a book.

"I'm here, Cap'n. But I reckon I'll soon be out, too!"

And he was right. For not much later the great Ranger was riding the golden sorrel toward the Rio Grande, once more to carry the law into remote regions of the State of Texas.